D1231794

NIGHT AND DANA

ANYA DAVIDSON

GRAPHIC UNIVERSE™ • MINNEAPOLIS

For Doris and Sherrie

Graphic Universe™
An imprint of Lerner Publishing Group, Inc.
241 First Avenue North
Minneapolis, MN 55401 USA

For reading levels and more information, look up this title at www.lernerbooks.com.

Design by Kimberly Morales.

Library of Congress Cataloging-in-Publication Data

Names: Davidson, Anya, author, artist.
Title: Night and Dana / Anya Davidson.
Description: Minneapolis, MN : Graphic Universe, [2023] | Audience: Ages 14–18 | Audience: Grades 10–12 | Summary: "When special-effects obsessives Dana and Lily begin work on an eco-horror movie, they realize they've been growing apart. But as everything starts going up in flames, Dana begins to forge her voice as a climate activist" —Provided by publisher.
Identifiers: LCCN 2022033748 (print) | LCCN 2022033749 (ebook) | ISBN 9781728430355 (library binding) | ISBN 9781728430362 (paperback) | ISBN 9781728494944 (ebook)
Subjects: CYAC: Graphic novels. | Friendship—Fiction. | Motion pictures—Production and direction—Fiction. | Self-realization—Fiction. | LCGFT: Graphic novels.
Classification: LCC PZ7.7.D375 Ni 2023 (print) | LCC PZ7.7.D375 (ebook) | DDC 741.5/973—dc23/eng/20220727

LC record available at https://lccn.loc.gov/2022033748
LC ebook record available at https://lccn.loc.gov/2022033749

Manufactured in the United States of America
1-49495-49539-1/11/2023

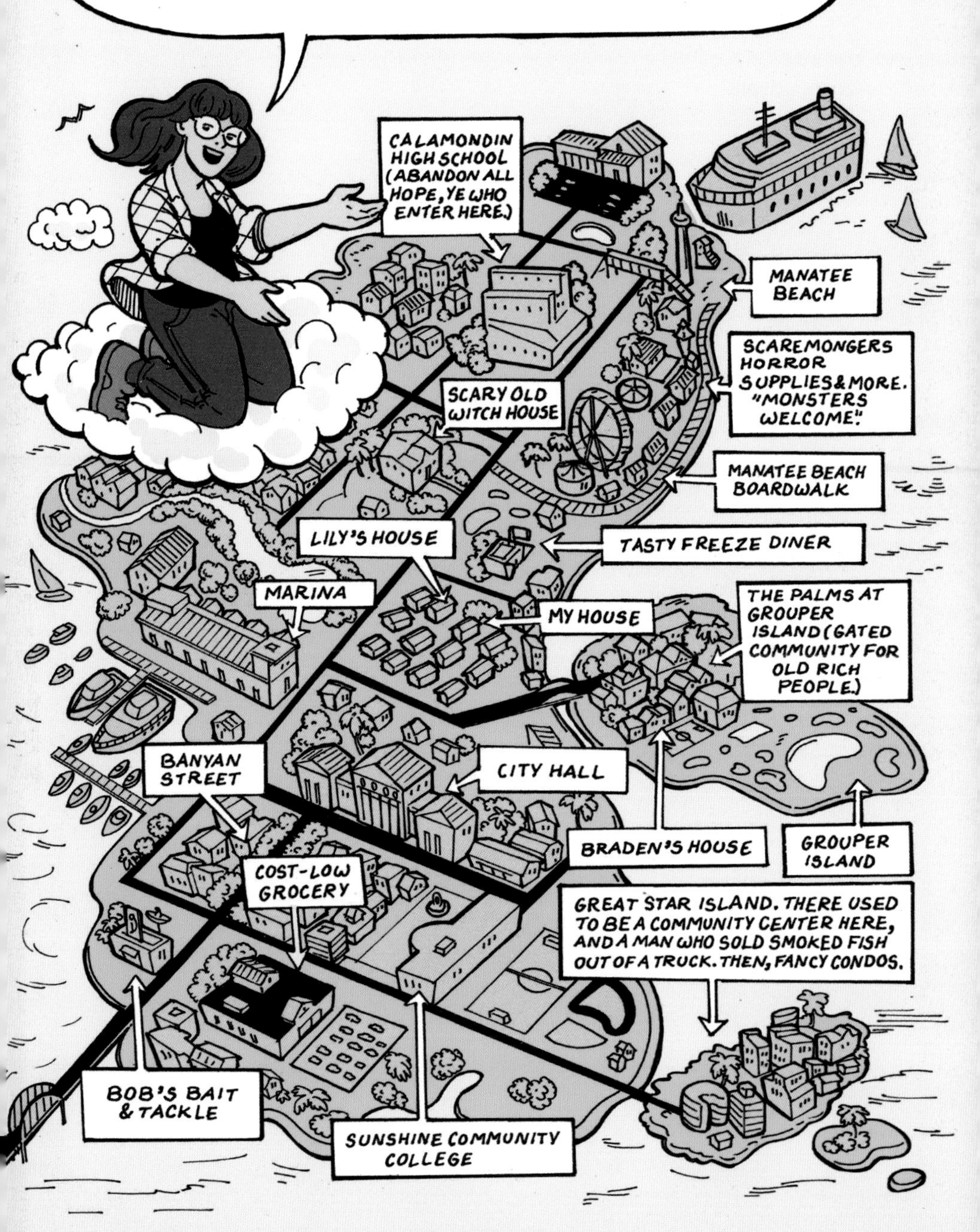
WELCOME TO BOCA BELLA, FLORIDA, POPULATION WHO CARES? I WASN'T BORN HERE - THE CLOSEST HOSPITAL IS ON THE MAINLAND, TWENTY MINUTES AWAY. IT'S NOT A BAD PLACE TO GROW UP, BUT BY AGE SEVENTEEN, I WAS DYING TO MAKE AN ESCAPE. TO A CITY WITH MUSEUMS AND THEATERS. A PLACE WHERE MONITOR LIZARDS DON'T EAT HOUSE PETS AND STOLEN GOLF CARTS AREN'T FRONT PAGE NEWS. IF YOU'RE A WEIRDO LIKE I AM, MAYBE YOU UNDERSTAND.
CALAMONDIN HIGH SCHOOL (ABANDON ALL HOPE, YE WHO ENTER HERE.)
MANATEE BEACH
SCAREMONGERS HORROR SUPPLIES & MORE. "MONSTERS WELCOME."
SCARY OLD WITCH HOUSE
MANATEE BEACH BOARDWALK
LILY'S HOUSE
TASTY FREEZE DINER
MARINA
MY HOUSE
THE PALMS AT GROUPER ISLAND (GATED COMMUNITY FOR OLD RICH PEOPLE.)
BANYAN STREET
CITY HALL
BRADEN'S HOUSE
GROUPER ISLAND
COST-LOW GROCERY
GREAT STAR ISLAND. THERE USED TO BE A COMMUNITY CENTER HERE, AND A MAN WHO SOLD SMOKED FISH OUT OF A TRUCK. THEN, FANCY CONDOS.
BOB'S BAIT & TACKLE
SUNSHINE COMMUNITY COLLEGE

CHAPTER ONE

IT WAS JANUARY OF OUR SENIOR YEAR, AND WHILE OUR CLASSMATES WERE PLANNING PROM PARTIES AND GRADUATION FETES, LILY AND I WERE PLOTTING A SERIES OF GRUESOME DEATHS. LIKE THE GREAT PHILOSOPHER MUHAMMAD ALI ONCE SAID, "DIFFERENT STROKES FOR DIFFERENT FOLKS."

SHARP TONGUE / COMES AS NO SURPRISE / ♪

I'M A MONSTER / M-M-M-M MONSTER / ♪

VROOM
CALAMONDIN HIGH SCHOOL

HEY, DYLAN.
HUH?

DANA! LOOK OUT!

CRACK

LILY? OH MY GOD, LILY, I DIDN'T SEE YOU.

OH MY GOD, ARE YOU OKAY?

AAH!
SOMEONE! HELP! PLEASE!
NOOO!

MISTER BOYSEN!

STAND BACK! DON'T TOUCH HER. YOU COULD DAMAGE HER SPINAL COLUMN.

OH MY GOD, THERE'S SOMETHING WRONG WITH HER EYE!

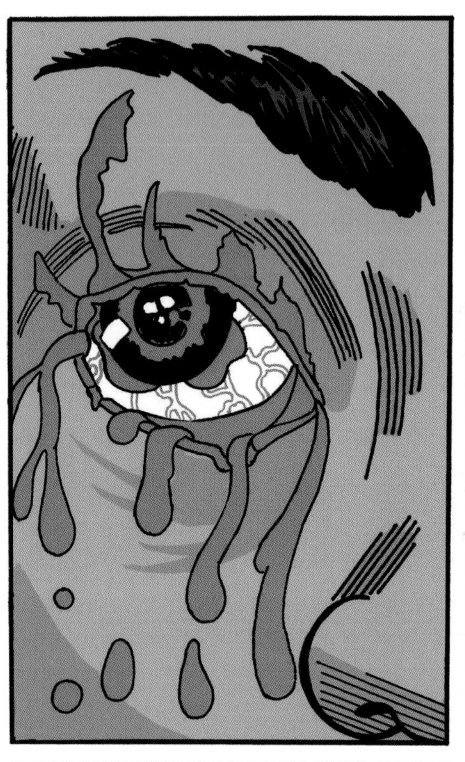

HELLO, 911? I'M IN THE PARKING LOT OF CALAMONDIN HIGH AND THERE'S BEEN AN ACCIDENT.

THE VICTIM IS LILLIAN VILLASEÑOR, AGED 17, AND SHE'S BEEN HIT BY A CAR.

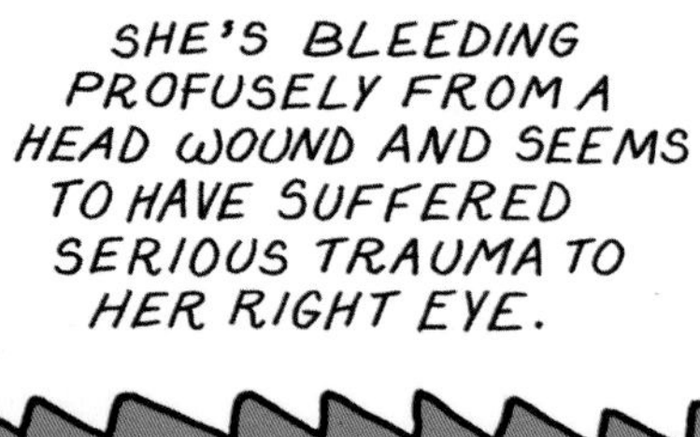
SHE'S BLEEDING PROFUSELY FROM A HEAD WOUND AND SEEMS TO HAVE SUFFERED SERIOUS TRAUMA TO HER RIGHT EYE.

YES, I CAN TAKE HER PULSE.
YES, I'LL STAY ON THE LINE.
LILY! ENOUGH!
CUT!

RIIIP
THANKS FOR
WATCHING!

LILY HAS NEVER HAD THE FEAR RESPONSE OF NORMAL MORTALS, BUT I WAS LOSING MY MIND...

WE'D BEEN WAITING TO LEAVE BOCA BELLA BASICALLY SINCE BEFORE WE WERE BORN, AND OUR PLAN WAS ROCK SOLID: GET SCHOLARSHIPS TO NYU, SHARE AN APARTMENT IN BROOKLYN, AND WORK IN DINERS WHILE WE BUILT OUR FOLLOWER COUNT.

PRINCIPAL LOBLAW HELD OUR ENTIRE FUTURE IN HER HANDS. SHE HAD MELLOWED OUT A LOT SINCE HER DIVORCE, BUT I WAS STILL JUSTIFIABLY FREAKED.

DIPLOMA
HAVE A SEAT.

TAP TAP

LILY, YOUR PARENTS ARE ON THEIR WAY.
UGH.
DIPLOMA

THEY TOLD ME YOU'VE BEEN USING AN APP TO POST VIDEOS OF YOURSELVES WITH FAKE INJURIES. I PULLED IT UP. IT'S QUITE POPULAR.
OH MY GOD.
CHAMPIONS
GIRL LOSES ARM IN SUPERMARKET

YOU COULD HAVE TRAUMATIZED YOUR CLASSMATES TODAY. NOT TO MENTION THAT A FALSE 911 EMERGENCY IS A MISDEMEANOR.

ARE YOU GONNA EXPEL US?
YOU BOTH CLEARLY HAVE A LOT OF CREATIVE ENERGY THAT NEEDS AN OUTLET.

MY FRIEND TEACHES FILM AT SUNSHINE COMMUNITY COLLEGE.
DIPLOMA

IT'S A CONTINUING STUDIES COURSE, OPEN TO STUDENTS OF ALL AGES. SHE'S AGREED TO LET YOU ENROLL.

IF YOU COMPLETE ALL OF THE ASSIGNMENTS- ON TOP OF YOUR REGULAR SCHOOLWORK- I'LL ALLOW YOU TO GRADUATE WITH THE REST OF YOUR CLASSMATES.

IF YOU SLIP UP? YOU'RE EXPELLED.

THANK YOU SO MUCH, PRINCIPAL LOBLAW.
I PROMISE WE WON'T MESS IT UP.

PROMISES ARE LIKE PIE CRUSTS.
DELICIOUS?

EASILY BROKEN.
GET OUT OF HERE.

CHAPTER TWO

UP UNTIL HIS FIFTH BIRTHDAY, MY BROTHER, JESSE, WAS LIKE A GARBAGE DISPOSAL. WE JOKED THAT HE WOULD EAT ANYTHING THAT DIDN'T MOVE.

THEN HE STARTED GOING THROUGH HIS PICKY PHASE. FOODS HE USED TO LOVE, ALL OF A SUDDEN HE WOULDN'T TOUCH.

I FELT LIKE STRANGLING HIM, WHICH MADE ME FEEL GUILTY, WHICH MADE ME EVEN MADDER. I STARTED TO DREAD MEALTIMES.

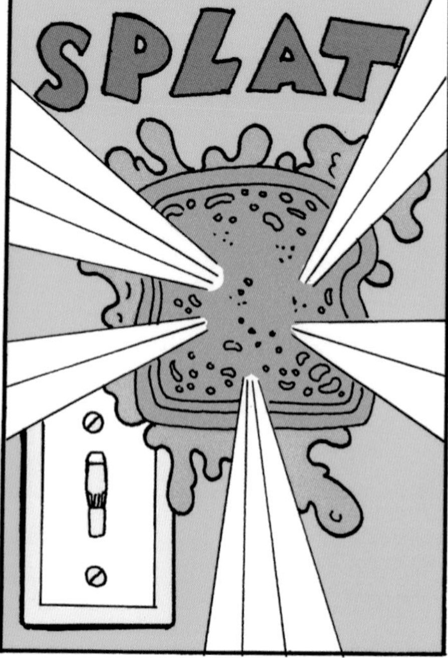

HAVE YOU EVER HEARD OF CUCKOO BIRDS? THEY'RE BROOD PARASITES. THEY LAY THEIR OWN EGGS IN OTHER BIRD'S NESTS. IT TRICKS THOSE BIRDS INTO HATCHING THEIR CHICKS FOR THEM.

MY MOM, JOANN, AND I ARE SO DIFFERENT, I'VE ALWAYS FELT LIKE I MUST HAVE BEEN HATCHED IN THE WRONG NEST.

I DON'T KNOW, JO. I SPEND MY WHOLE LIFE BABYSITTING. MAYBE FIND SOMEONE ELSE TO BABYSIT FOR ONCE.
YEAH, WELL, I SPEND MY WHOLE LIFE WORKING TO KEEP A ROOF OVER YOUR HEAD.

IF YOU HATE IT SO MUCH, MAYBE STOP HAVING KIDS.

SLAM
FUNERAL

JO'S BOYFRIEND, BRYAN, HAS THE CHARISMA OF A SOGGY BREADSTICK. SHE MET HIM AT THE SALON WHEN SHE WAS CUTTING HIS (NOW EX-) WIFE'S HAIR, SO NEEDLESS TO SAY HE'S A DOG. NOT SURPRISING, CONSIDERING JO'S TRACK RECORD, BUT DISAPPOINTING, WHEN YOU HAVE SO FEW ADULT ROLE MODELS.

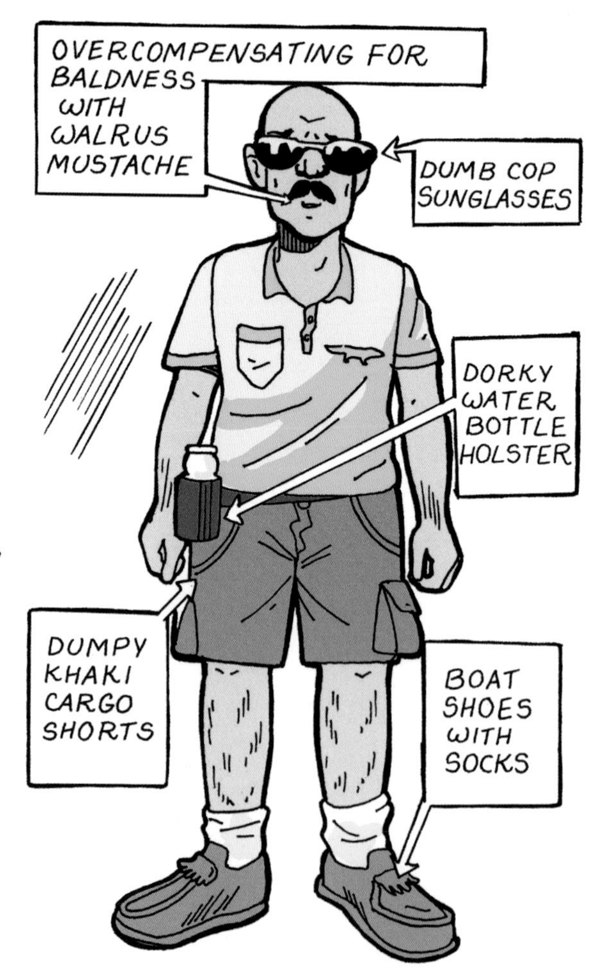

BRADEN NASH SAT NEXT TO US IN EIGHTH GRADE BIOLOGY AND NEVER REALLY LEFT.

BY THEN, LILY AND I ALREADY HAD A REPUTATION. OTHER KIDS CALLED US THE TERROR TWINS AND KEPT THEIR DISTANCE.

FROM WHAT WE COULD TELL, BRADEN WAS PRETTY NORMAL. HE WAS INTO SOCCER AND CARS AND THE GIRLS IN BIKINIS ON THE COVERS OF CAR MAGAZINES.

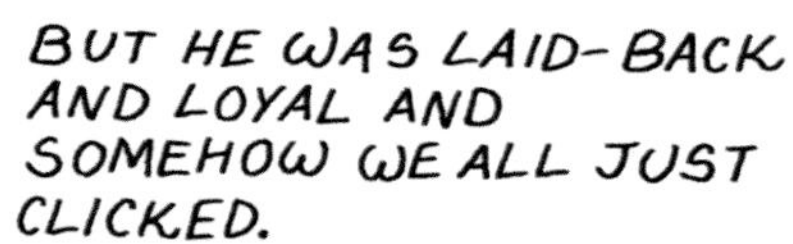
BUT HE WAS LAID-BACK AND LOYAL AND SOMEHOW WE ALL JUST CLICKED.

YOU COMING TO THE LOWRIDER SHOW ON SATURDAY?
WE CAN'T, BRADEN. WE'RE BEING PUNISHED, REMEMBER?
THAT'S THE DAY WE START OUR MOVIE CLASS.

MY FRIEND MIKE TOOK THAT CLASS LAST SEMESTER. HE SAID IT WAS BRUTAL.
MIKE'S AN IDIOT.
THAT'S KINDA TRUE.

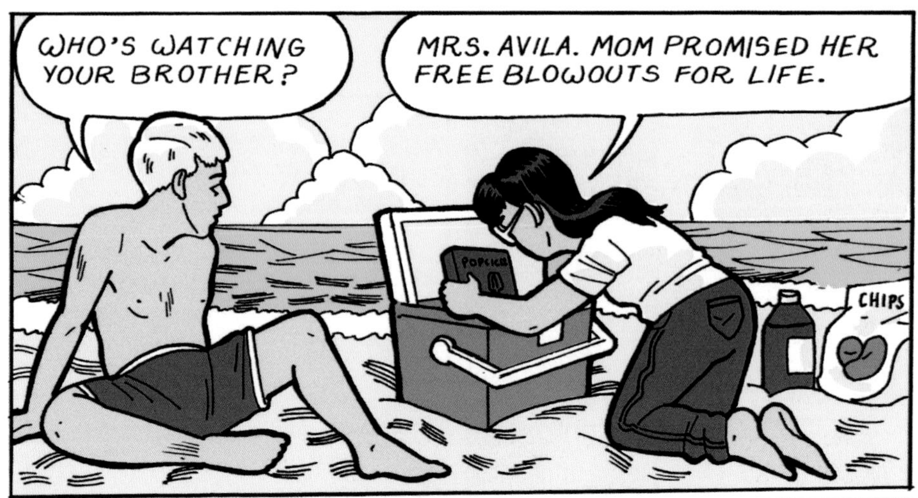
WHO'S WATCHING YOUR BROTHER?
MRS. AVILA. MOM PROMISED HER FREE BLOWOUTS FOR LIFE.
POPSICLE
CHIPS

SHE'S LIKE EIGHTY-FIVE.

IS THAT SAFE? I HEARD SHE GOT LOST IN THE COST-LOW PARKING LOT LAST WEEKEND.
SUN BLOCK

SHUT UP. IT'LL BE FINE.

CHAPTER THREE

I LOVE WEIRDOS LIKE OTHER PEOPLE LOVE ICE CREAM, SO THE FIRST TIME WE PASSED THE MEGAPHONE LADY ON THE WAY TO SATURDAY CLASS, I'LL ADMIT, I WAS INTRIGUED.

THE GHOULS AT CITY HALL SIT IN THEIR AIR-CONDITIONED OFFICES DAY AFTER DAY, APPROVING PERMITS FOR CONDOS AND HOTELS AND STRIP-MALL DEVELOPMENTS.

WELL, I SAY, GET OUT, MALEVOLENT SPIRITS, BE GONE! BY THE POWER OF THE GODDESS HECATE, I BANISH YOU FROM THIS BUILDING!

CRACK
CITY HALL

SHE IS A **LOT**.
I LIKE HER.
CITY HAL

IF YOU CAN'T AFFORD TO LEAVE BOCA BELLA BUT YOU DON'T WANT TO WORK AS A LANDSCAPER, HOUSEKEEPER, OR A SERVER, YOU GO TO SUNSHINE COLLEGE TO LEARN TO BE A HOTEL MANAGER OR A RESTAURANT MANAGER OR A NURSE.

ANY FANTASIES YOU HAVE ABOUT CAMPUS ARCHITECTURE- SPIRAL STAIRCASES WITH CARVED WOODEN BANNISTERS, IVY-COVERED CONSERVATORIES, TURRETED CLOCK TOWERS - COME HERE TO DIE.

THANKS TO ALL OF YOU FOR COMING OUT ON SUCH A MISERABLE DAY. MY NAME IS JEANINE ROGERS. I'M YOUR INSTRUCTOR.
I BEGAN MY CAREER AT BBTV, THE PUBLIC ACCESS STATION HERE IN BOCA BELLA. I MOVED TO LOS ANGELES, WHERE I WORKED IN FILM AND TELEVISION FOR OVER A DECADE.
internal microphone
view finder
Camera Body
ME (JEANINE)

I'M THE DIRECTOR OF THREE INDIE HORROR FILMS, "VOIDCRAWLERS," "UPRISE," "CROSSROADS SONG," ABOUT THE BLUES SINGER ROBERT JOHNSON, WHICH WON AN AUDIENCE AWARD AT SUNDANCE.

LET'S START BY GOING AROUND THE ROOM. EVERYONE PLEASE SHARE YOUR NAME, YOUR PRONOUNS, IF YOU FEEL COMFORTABLE, AND TELL US WHY YOU SIGNED UP FOR THIS CLASS.

MY NAME IS JAKE HOSKINS. I'M A RETIRED COMMERCIAL AIRLINE PILOT, AND I SIGNED UP FOR THIS CLASS SO I CAN MAKE VIDEOS OF MY BABY GRANDNIECE.
ME (JEANINE)

I'M WYE. W-Y-E, LIKE THE OAK, NOT THE QUESTION. MY PRONOUNS ARE THEY / THEM.

I GRADUATED FROM SEA GRAPE HIGH LAST YEAR, AND I'VE BEEN WORKING AT THE BEACH MART.

I'M SAVING UP FOR ART SCHOOL, BUT I FIGURED I'D GET AS MANY CREDITS AS POSSIBLE AT COMMUNITY COLLEGE.

SMACK

OW.
I'M DANA. SHE / HER.

ME AND MY FRIEND GOT IN TROUBLE AT SCHOOL AND WERE FORCED TO SIGN UP FOR THIS CLASS.

YOUR PRINCIPAL AND I USED TO SNEAK CIGARETTES OUT OF HER MOTHER'S PURSE AND SMOKE THEM BEHIND WORREL'S MARINA. PLEASE TELL HER I SAID HELLO.

NOW THAT YOU HAVE A FEEL FOR THE CAMERAS, THE NEXT THING I WANT TO COVER IS HOW TO FRAME YOUR SHOTS.

IS ANYONE FAMILIAR WITH THE RULE OF THIRDS?

WYE? CAN YOU DEMONSTRATE ON THE BOARD?
SURE.

CLOSE YOUR MOUTH OR YOU'LL CATCH FLIES.

YOUR FIRST ASSIGNMENT IS TO COME IN NEXT WEEK WITH 16 EXAMPLES OF NICELY FRAMED SHOTS.

I WANT YOU TO DEMONSTRATE THAT YOU'RE COMFORTABLE USING THE TRIPOD AND THAT YOU UNDERSTAND COLOR BALANCE, FOCUS, AND EXPOSURE.

HEY, DO YOU TWO RUN A VIDEO CHANNEL CALLED "BLOOD BRAINS"?

YEAH, THAT'S US.
THOSE POSTS ARE HILARIOUS!

THAT ONE WHERE YOU PULLED YOUR ARM OFF IN THE COST-LOW BABY AISLE... HOW DID YOU EVEN DO THAT?

I JUST MADE A CAST OF HER REAL ARM IN FOAM LATEX.

I BOUGHT A BOOK AT SCAREMONGER'S AND TAUGHT MYSELF HOW.

SCAREMONGER'S- THE COMIC SHOP ON THE BOARDWALK?
THEY SELL ALL KINDS OF STUFF-COMICS, DOLLS, MOVIES.

TWICE A YEAR THEY TEACH A SPECIAL EFFECTS MAKEUP CLASS AND THEY CARRY ALL THE SUPPLIES.
PIZZAPUFFS

I'M STARVING-WANT A HOTDOG?
NO THANKS.
NAH, BUT WE'LL WAIT WITH YOU.
DIRTY DOGS

HEY- WHY DO YOU THINK A DIRECTOR LIKE JEANINE ROGERS IS TEACHING AT SUNSHINE COLLEGE?
I DON'T KNOW. MAYBE SHE'S RETIRED.
DOGS

HI. CAN I GET THE SEOUL SENSATION VEGGIE DOG WITH NO MAYO?

OH. THAT'S HELLA GOOD.

I DON'T THINK JEANINE'S RETIRED. SHE LOOKS FORTY, MAX.

MAYBE SHE'S AN ALCOHOLIC.
MAYBE HER HUSBAND WAS A STUNTMAN AND HE DIED ON SET IN A TRAGIC MOTORCYCLE ACCIDENT.
AND TO COPE WITH THE GRIEF SHE MOVED...HERE? NO ONE MOVES HERE EXCEPT TO RETIRE.

HEY, DO YOU WANT TO ALL HANG OUT AND DO OUR HOMEWORK TOGETHER?

SURE. WHEN WERE YOU THINKING? I'M AT THE BEACH MART MONDAY THROUGH FRIDAY 'TIL SEVEN.

TUESDAY AT EIGHT?
I HAVE TO BABYSIT.

YOU CAN BRING JESSE.
NO, THAT'S HIS BEDTIME.
WELCOME BACK

OKAY, WELL, NEVER MIND.
NO, YOU TWO GO AHEAD. I CAN GET THOSE SHOTS ON MY OWN.

I'M STILL DOWN IF YOU'RE DOWN, WYE.

AND JUST LIKE THAT, MY BEST FRIEND IN THE WHOLE WORLD BETRAYED ME UNFORGIVABLY. THE FACT THAT I MIGHT HAVE DONE THE SAME THING IN HER PLACE—WYE IS, OBJECTIVELY, A TOTAL BABE—NEVER CROSSED MY MIND.
I LAUGHED IT OFF, BUT INSIDE IT FELT LIKE I'D BEEN SHOT WITH A HARPOON GUN. TO MAKE MATTERS WORSE, LILY ACED THAT ASSIGNMENT.

HOW'S THE CLASS GOING?
LILY'S KILLING IT.
WHAT? YOU'RE CRAZY.

SHE GOT AN A+ ON OUR FIRST ASSIGNMENT. JEANINE SAID SHE HAS A NATURAL EYE FOR COMPOSITION. PEOPLE WERE **SHOCKED** BY HOW GOOD SHE IS.

WHERE DID YOU SHOOT?
AT THE SKATE PARK.

WITH WYE.

THE EMO KID FROM SEA GRAPE?
THEY'RE NOT EMO. THEY'RE TOTALLY THEIR OWN THING. THAT'S WHY THEY'RE COOL.

LILY'S IN LOVE.
SHUT UP!

OUR NEXT ASSIGNMENT IS TO PROFILE A LOCAL BUSINESS.

YOU CAN COME BUG ME AT THE AUTO SHOP.
I WAS THINKING OF INTERVIEWING RON AT SCAREMONGERS.

WHAT BUSINESS ARE YOU DOING, DANA?
MAYBE MOM'S SALON? I WANT TO DO BOB'S BAIT & TACKLE, BUT I'M AFRAID TO ASK IF I CAN FILM IN THERE. BOB IS KIND OF INTENSE.

I CAN GO WITH YOU.
ARE YOU SURE?

YEAH, WE CAN GO AFTER SCHOOL TOMORROW.

YOU'RE SURE YOU'RE SURE?
I NEED A BIRTHDAY PRESENT FOR MY DAD. HE LOVES THAT PLACE.
HIGH WINDS TODAY

CHAPTER FOUR

EVEN THOUGH WE HUNG OUT ALL THE TIME, I'D NEVER SPENT TIME ALONE WITH JUST BRADEN. IT WAS KIND OF AWKWARD BUT EXCITING TOO. IT FELT WRONG, BUT I COULDN'T TELL IF IT WAS BAD WRONG OR GOOD WRONG.

I WROTE MY NYU ENTRANCE ESSAY ABOUT BOB'S.
WHAT WAS THE QUESTION?

DISCUSS A WORK OF ART THAT MADE A LASTING IMPRESSION ON YOU. I CHOSE THE SIGN.

"CATCH ME AT BOB'S"

SERIOUSLY?

WHEN'S THE LAST TIME YOU SET FOOT IN AN ART MUSEUM? THIS SIGN IS A PART OF OUR LIVES. WE PASS BY IT EVERY DAY.

ISN'T NYU YOUR DREAM SCHOOL? SOUNDS LIKE YOU TOOK A BIG RISK.
BIG RISKS, BIG REWARDS.

HOW WAS BOB'S?
IT WAS GOOD. PRETTY EASY.

BRADEN WAS KIND OF SQUICKED OUT BY THE WORMS. HE SAID HE HATES ANYTHING WITHOUT LEGS. WHAT'S UP WITH YOU AND WYE?

I THINK WE'RE KIND OF DATING.
SHE SAID, SURPRISING NO ONE.

WEAK!

DINNER'S READY.

COMING!

GUSTAVO VILLASEÑOR IS A MARINE MECHANIC AND A REALLY GOOD COOK, BUT HIS DREAM IN LIFE WAS TO BE A TV WRITER.

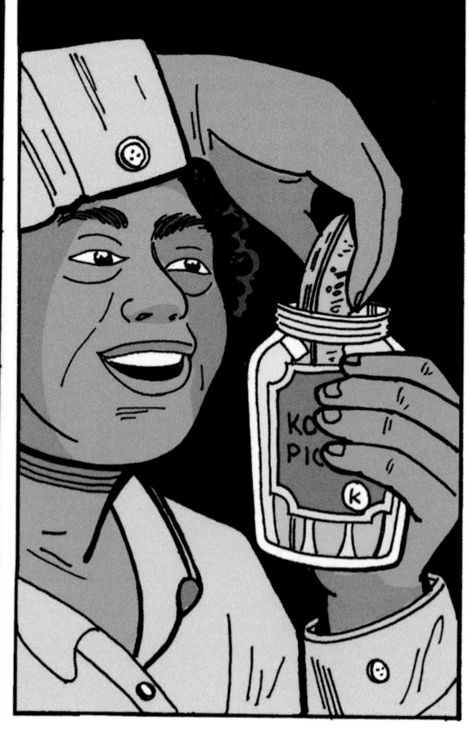

ONCE, WHEN WE WERE TRYING ON HER MOM'S HIGH HEELS, LILY FOUND A SPEC SCRIPT FOR AN EPISODE OF "WARP WIZARDS" HIDDEN IN A SHOE BOX.

WHEN WE ASKED GUSTAVO ABOUT IT, HE WAS SUPER EMBARRASSED, BUT I KNOW HE'S PART OF THE REASON LILY'S SO INTO FILMMAKING.

CHECK OUT MEGAPHONE LADY.
WHAT'S IN THE WHEELBARROW? IT SMELLS LIKE DEATH.
CITY H

THE GREAT GODDESS IS ANGRY. SHE CRIES OUT FOR RETRIBUTION.

BUT IT'S NOT TOO LATE TO MAKE A CHANGE. LIGHT SHINES BRIGHTEST IN THE DARKNESS.

FLOWERS GROW TALLEST WHEN THEY'RE PLANTED IN SHIT!

OW. MY EARS.
SHRIEK

ALRIGHT, LET'S GIVE LILY'S WORK OUR FULL ATTENTION. DANA, CAN YOU HIT THE LIGHTS?
CLACK
CLACK
CLACK
MONSTERS WELCOME

I WAS ALWAYS KIND OF A MORBID KID. I GREW UP WATCHING OLD B MOVIES LATE AT NIGHT ON CHANNEL 21.

I STARTED OUT MAKING MONSTERS IN MY GARAGE OUT OF FOAM LATEX AND SHAG CARPET.

NOW MOST SPECIAL EFFECTS ARE DONE DIGITALLY. BUT YOUR EYE KNOWS THE DIFFERENCE.

IN THE BACK OF YOUR MIND, YOU ALWAYS KNOW. PRACTICAL EFFECTS - PUPPETS, SUITS, PROSTHETICS - THAT STUFF IS REAL.

YOU CAN DO ANYTHING WITH A COMPUTER BUT WHERE'S THE CHALLENGE IN THAT?
DISCOUNT COMICS

EXCELLENT WORK, LILY. VERY SMART TO INTERCUT THE INTERVIEW WITH FOUND FOOTAGE. AS MUCH AS POSSIBLE, YOU WANT TO AVOID TALKING-HEAD SHOTS.

I SHOULD HAVE KNOWN LILY'S SCAREMONGER'S PROFILE WOULD BE A MASTERPIECE, CONSIDERING HOW WELL SHE DID ON OUR FIRST ASSIGNMENT. SOME PEOPLE JUST FIND THEIR THING AND IT CLICKS.
KING KONG

DON'T GET ME WRONG– I WAS HAPPY FOR HER. I WAS JUST STARTING TO WONDER WHEN I WAS GOING TO FIND **MY** THING.

THE BOCA BELLA FILM FESTIVAL IS COMING UP AND THERE'S A CATEGORY FOR SHORT FILMS.

YOUR SUBMISSION COULD BE AS LITTLE AS TEN OR FIFTEEN MINUTES LONG.
7th ANNUAL Boca Bella FILM FESTIVAL
SANDCASTLE THEATER
SATURDAY, MAY 23
GENERAL ADMISSION $10

IT'S ONLY MID-FEBRUARY— YOU'VE GOT PLENTY OF TIME. I THINK YOU THREE SHOULD SERIOUSLY CONSIDER ENTERING.
REALLY?

THE WINNING ENTRY LAST YEAR WAS ABOUT A TALKING SEAGULL. I THINK THE BAR IS PRETTY LOW.

OH, YOU DEFINITELY HAVE A SHOT.

COULD WE MAKE A HORROR MOVIE?

SURE.
THEN YES! LET'S DO IT!

AMAZING.

FOR A GROUP OF KIDS THAT SPENT OUR CHILDHOODS READING ABOUT SPONTANEOUS HUMAN COMBUSTION AND BROOD PARASITES, WE HAD A SURPRISINGLY HARD TIME COMING UP WITH A HORROR MOVIE PREMISE.
OKAY, WHAT IF, UM, DEMONS COME TO EARTH AND THEY LOOK JUST LIKE REGULAR PEOPLE BUT THEY'RE SECRETLY BUILDING A SOUL-SUCKING MACHINE.

THAT'S THE EXACT PLOT OF "BLANK STARE."
NO, LISTEN-
CHIPS

WHAT IF THERE'S A WORLD WHERE EVERYONE IS BORN WITH TELEPATHIC ABILITIES, AND THEN ONE BOY ISN'T AND HE'S HUNTED FOR BEING DIFFERENT.

THAT'S THE EXACT PLOT OF AN EPISODE OF "WARP WIZARDS." WE WATCHED IT TOGETHER LAST WEEK.
EVERY IDEA HAS BEEN DONE ALREADY. YOU JUST HAVE TO TAKE ONE AND MAKE IT YOUR OWN.

WE'RE NEVER GOING TO GET ANYTHING DONE IN THIS HEAT. LET'S GO TO THE BEACH.
WE? SO YOU ARE GOING TO HELP US?

I SAID I WOULD. I JUST DON'T HAVE ANY A-V SKILLS.
JUST DO WHAT WE TELL YOU AND YOU'LL BE FINE.
YES MA'AM.

CAUTION BOATERS

SNIFF SNIFF
I RECOGNIZE THAT SMELL.

FROM THE COURTHOUSE. OH, THAT IS AWFUL.
RED TIDE'S SUPPOSED TO BE WORSE THAN EVER THIS YEAR.

HEY! WYE! WHERE ARE YOU GOING?

I WANT TO SEE FOR MYSELF.

WAIT FOR ME!

WE'D GROWN UP WITH RED TIDE. IT'S CAUSED BY KARENIA BREVIS, A KIND OF ALGAE HARMFUL TO MARINE LIFE. IT HAPPENED OCCASIONALLY IN LATE SUMMER, TURNING THE WATER A PINKISH RED.
DANGER
RED TIDE
7

RED TIDE THRIVES IN WARM WATER, SO OCEAN WARMING HAS EXTENDED ITS GROWING CYCLE.

PLUS, FERTILIZER RUNOFF FROM FACTORY FARMS HAS BEEN FEEDING THE ALGAE, CAUSING BIGGER BLOOMS THAN EVER BEFORE.

BASICALLY, WHAT USED TO BE A BRIEF NUISANCE HAS TURNED INTO A YEARLY, MONTHS-LONG HORROR SHOW.

THERE GOES SPRING BREAK.
OH! POOR PUPPIES.
WAY TO GO, HUMANS. GREAT JOB EXISTING ON THE PLANET. REALLY. A+.
HEY— WHAT IF WE MADE A DOCUMENTARY ABOUT THE RED TIDE?

THAT'S NOT A BAD IDEA, BUT WE NEED TO PRACTICE OUR SCREENWRITING SKILLS.
HOW ABOUT ECO-HORROR? SOMEONE GETS THROWN INTO POLLUTED WATER AND THEY COME OUT ALL MONSTERFIED.
THAT'S KIND OF GENIUS, ACTUALLY. WYE, LETS TAKE YOUR LAPTOP TO THE LIBRARY.

BIG YES TO AIR-CONDITIONING.
I'M GOING TO WORK. CATCH YOU DORKS LATER.

YOU LOVE US.
I LOVE YOU, AND YOU ARE DORKS. BOTH OF THOSE THINGS ARE TRUE.

I GOT A FUNNY FEELING WHEN I FLIRTED WITH BRADEN. IT HAD BEEN HAPPENING MORE AND MORE SINCE WINTER BREAK. IT WAS NICE, BUT I WASN'T SURE HOW FAR I WANTED TO TAKE IT.

WHAT ABOUT MERMAIDS?
MERMAIDS AREN'T SCARY.
MERMAIDS ARE TERRIFYING.

HARROW'S
OCCULT COMPENDIUM
YOUR GUIDE TO EVERYTHING THAT CLAWS, BITES & GOES BUMP IN THE NIGHT.

Siren: In Greek mythology, sailors plugged their ears or risked being lured to their deaths by the ethereal voices of these dangerous sea monsters.
Mami Wata: venerated in western, central, and southern Africa, as well as parts of the African diaspora. Has benevolent as well as malevolent aspects. May cause or cure a number of ailments, including sterility, and has been known to both save and drown errant swimmers. Often depicted holding snakes.

Abyzou: a Sumerian demon with the tail of a serpent. Lived in primordial waters. Associated with jealousy and miscarriages.

OKAY I STAND CORRECTED. MERMAIDS ARE SCARY AS HELL.
READING IS MAGIC

CITY HALL
YOU CAN'T HIDE FROM THE REDTIDE

FROM THE REDTIDE

HOW'S THE SCRIPT COMING?
WE JUST FINISHED THE OUTLINE.
GIVE ME YOUR ELEVATOR PITCH.
OUR WHAT?

SELL IT TO ME. PRETEND I'M A PRODUCER WHO JUST STEPPED INTO AN ELEVATOR WITH YOU.
I CAN'T. IT'S TOO MUCH PRESSURE.

YOU'VE GOT TO HAVE A THICK SKIN TO BE IN THIS BUSINESS. IF YOU CAN'T HANDLE CONSTRUCTIVE CRITICISM, YOU'RE TOAST.

DAAANG. OKAY... RAIN ROBERTS MOVES TO BOCA BELLA WITH HER MOM, A MARINE BIOLOGIST WHO'S STUDYING OCEAN WARMING.

SHE HAS A THING FOR DEREK, A POPULAR RICH KID. THEY HOOK UP ONE NIGHT AT A PARTY, BUT THE NEXT DAY AT SCHOOL, HE ACTS LIKE HE DOESN'T KNOW HER.

ONE NIGHT, DEREK INVITES RAIN TO GO OUT ON HIS BOAT, BUT IT'S A PRANK. WHEN SHE GETS THERE, DEREK AND ALL HIS FRIENDS THROW HER OVERBOARD.
BUT THE WATER'S FILTHY, FULL OF TOXIC CHEMICALS.
RAIN STARTS TO CHANGE. SHE GROWS GILLS AND FINS AND CRAWLS BACK INTO THE OCEAN.

WHERE SHE LURES DEREK AND HIS FRIENDS TO THEIR DEATHS WITH HER SIREN SONG.

IT'S KIND OF LIKE "PROM NIGHT MASSACRE" MEETS "CREATURE FROM 1000 FATHOMS."

WELL, I'M NOT A BIG-TIME PRODUCER, BUT I DO HAVE... A LAUNDRY TICKET AND AN AFTER-DINNER MINT.
YOU LIKE IT?

I ALWAYS LIKE IT WHEN A MONSTER GETS TO TELL THEIR SIDE OF THE STORY.

CHAPTER FIVE

ONCE THE SCRIPT WAS WRITTEN, WE STARTED PREPRODUCTION, WHICH IS BASICALLY A LOT OF PLANNING SO YOU DON'T WASTE TIME WHEN THE CAMERAS ROLL. I WAS LOOKING FORWARD TO DESIGNING THE COSTUMES OR DRAWING THE STORYBOARDS, BUT GUESS WHO GOT THOSE JOBS.

SHUT UP. THEY'RE AMAZING. SHOW THEM THE MUTATION SCENE.

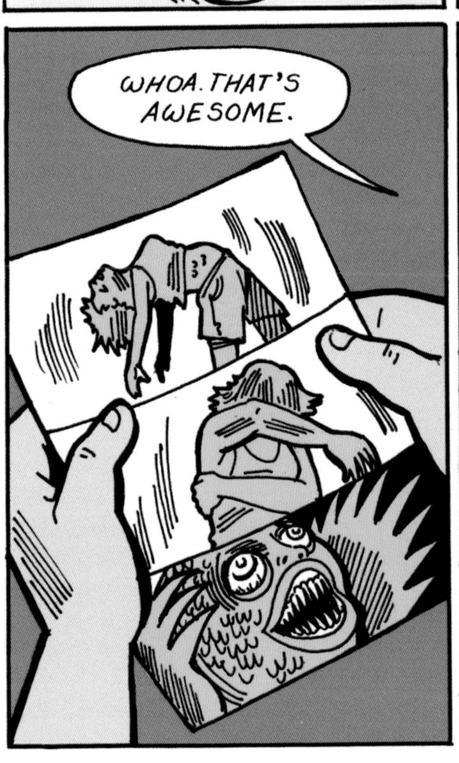
WHOA. THAT'S AWESOME.

I WANT TO SEE.

BRADEN, I NEED YOU TO GO OVER THE SCRIPT BREAKDOWN AND MAKE A LIST OF ALL THE PROPS WE NEED FOR EACH SCENE.
WHAT ABOUT ME? I CAN'T GET STARTED ON THE MONSTER MAKEUP UNTIL WE'VE CAST RAIN.

YOU CAN BE OUR... LOCATION SCOUT.
NO WAY. GET BRADEN TO DO IT, AND I'LL DO PROPS.
DANA!
WHAT? I HATE TALKING TO PEOPLE.

YOU'RE TALKING TO US.
YEAH. IT'S EXHAUSTING.

WYE'S BROTHER ALREADY SAID WE COULD BORROW HIS BOAT.

WE JUST NEED A PLACE TO FILM THE INTERIOR SCENES.

IT'S GOTTA BE SOMEWHERE HELLA SPOOKY, LIKE THE WITCH HOUSE ON CALAMONDIN HILL.

SINCE WHEN DO YOU SAY "HELLA"?

NOW LILY WAS COPYING WYE'S SPEECH PATTERNS. IT REMINDED ME OF THE EPISODE OF "WARP WIZARDS" WHERE A NEW GIRL COMES TO SCHOOL AND ALL THE OTHER LITTLE GIRLS START DRESSING LIKE HER AND TALKING LIKE HER, AND THEN THEY FORM A GANG AND MURDER THEIR PARENTS.

NEVER MIND. I TAKE BACK EVERYTHING I SAID BEFORE. ONE NICE GESTURE FROM LILY AND I WAS READY TO WALK BLINDFOLDED INTO A NEST OF RATTLESNAKES FOR HER.

THE WITCH HOUSE WAS KIND OF A NEIGHBORHOOD LANDMARK.

FOR MOST OF MY LIFE, THERE WAS A FOR SALE SIGN IN THE FRONT YARD, AND THEN ONE DAY IT WAS GONE.

NO WORKERS EVER CAME TO FIX THE PLACE UP, BUT WE STARTED TO NOTICE LIGHTS ON AT NIGHT. IT WAS OVERGROWN AND A BIT TRAGIC– THE PERFECT SET FOR A HORROR SHORT.

HELLO?

IT'S YOU. FROM CITY HALL. WITH THE MEGAPHONE.

I DON'T LIVE THERE, THANK GODDESS. YOU WANT A DRINK?

I CAME TO ASK YOU SOMETHING. MY FRIENDS AND I ARE MAKING A SHORT FILM. WE LOVE YOUR HOUSE AND WE WERE WONDERING IF WE COULD SHOOT SOME SCENES HERE.

IS IT A LOVE STORY? I'M DAPHNE OCEAN, BY THE WAY.
DANA DRUCKER. IT'S A HORROR FILM ACTUALLY. ECO-HORROR. INSPIRED BY THE RED TIDE.

ARTHUR AND I USED TO GO TO THE DOLLAR DRIVE-IN TO SEE EVERY CREATURE FEATURE ON OPENING NIGHT.

I'VE GOTTEN SENTIMENTAL IN MY OLD AGE, THOUGH. DOES YOUR STORY HAVE A HAPPY ENDING?

DEPENDS ON YOUR DEFINITION OF "HAPPY."
HMMM. WELL OF COURSE YOU CAN FILM HERE.

WE'LL PROBABLY BE LOUD. WE'LL HAVE TO MOVE THINGS AROUND. WE MIGHT HAVE TO SHOOT LATE AT NIGHT.
THAT'S ALRIGHT. YOU MAY HAVE THE TOTAL RUN OF THE HOUSE.

I ONLY ASK THAT YOU PLEASE STEER CLEAR OF THIS ROOM.
YEAH, SURE.

IF YOU'RE CONCERNED ABOUT THE RED TIDE, ANCHORWATCH, AN ENVIRONMENTAL GROUP I VOLUNTEER WITH, IS HOLDING A CLIMATE RALLY ON SUNDAY AFTERNOON.

THANKS. I'VE, UH, GOT PLANS WITH MY FRIEND. MAYBE ANOTHER TIME, THOUGH.
HERE'S A FLYER IN CASE YOU CHANGE YOUR MIND.

I JUST DON'T LIKE THE IDEA OF YOU FILMING IN THAT WOMAN'S HOUSE.
WE HAVEN'T STARTED FILMING. WE'RE STILL IN PREPRODUCTION.
DANA, SHE COULD BE DANGEROUS.

WHATEVER, BRYAN.
SHE COULD HAVE A DRUG PROBLEM. SHE COULD BE MENTALLY ILL.
RIGHT. BECAUSE EVERYONE WHO DRESSES FUNNY IS MENTALLY ILL.

YOU'VE SEEN HER HEXING CITY HALL. SHE'S A NUTCASE.
BECAUSE SHE'S WORRIED ABOUT BOCA BELLA SINKING UNDERWATER?

THERE'S ALWAYS BEEN FLOODING ON THE SOUTHERN COAST OF FLORIDA, DANA. IT'S PART OF A NATURAL CYCLE THAT HAS NOTHING TO DO WITH HUMAN ACTIVITY.
WOW, BRYAN. I THOUGHT YOU SOLD CAR INSURANCE. I DIDN'T REALIZE YOU WERE A CLIMATE SCIENTIST.
FRANKENSTEIN

DANA, THAT'S IT. YOU'RE NOT COMING ON OUR BOAT TRIP.

WHAT BOAT TRIP? NO ONE EVER TELLS ME ANYTHING!

WE'RE SAILING TO THE KEYS AND SPENDING SPRING BREAK AT MY TIME-SHARE.

SINCE WHEN DO YOU SAIL?
I'VE BEEN TAKING LESSONS.

WELL, I'D RATHER STICK FORKS IN MY EYES THAN BE STUCK ON A BOAT WITH YOU IDIOTS.

I GUESS YOU'LL BE SPENDING SPRING BREAK ALONE, THEN.
OH NO. UNSUPERVISED DURING SPRING BREAK. EVERY TEENAGER'S WORST NIGHTMARE.

CALAMONDIN STRONG!
SPIRIT WEEK SIGN-UP
BIOLOGY

TRACK TRYOUTS
COUNSELOR ROOM 202
OPEN CASTING CALL
OUT OF WATER
A SHORT FILM DIRECTED BY LILY VILLASEÑOR
SATURDAY, FEB 15
CALAMONDIN HIGH AUDITORIUM
*FREE COOKIES WHILE SUPPLIES LAST.
SIT STAY READ
YOGA

YOU SHOULD AUDITION, TREASURE.
I'VE NEVER ACTED BEFORE.

THAT DOESN'T MATTER.
I GET NERVOUS IN FRONT OF PEOPLE.

YOU COMPETE ON THE SWIM TEAM!
THAT'S DIFFERENT.
NOT THAT ALL DIFFERENT.

GIVE IT A SHOT. THERE'LL BE COOKIES.
I CAN'T HAVE COOKIES. COACH HAS ME ON A KETO DIET.

MAKING A MOVIE, HUH? LET ME KNOW IF YOU NEED ANY EXTRAS FOR THE SEX SCENES.
WE'RE GOOD, DYLAN. THANKS, THOUGH.

YOU KNOW WHERE TO FIND ME IF YOU CHANGE YOUR MIND.

WHAT A CLOWN.

WHO SHOULD WE ASK TO AUDITION FOR THE ROLE OF DEREK?
BRADEN'S KIND OF A JOCK. I THOUGHT HE COULD DO IT.

HA! YOU REALLY THOUGHT I WAS INTO YOU? YOU ARE DELUSIONAL, RAIN!

COOKIES

DEREK. WHY ARE YOU DOING THIS?
UM, BECAUSE I WAS BORED AND YOU WERE ALWAYS AROUND?

LIKE A HOUSEFLY
WAITING TO GET
ZAPPED.

COME ON, DEREK.
JUST LET ME OFF
THE BOAT.
YOU HEAR THAT?
SHE WANTS OFF
THE BOAT!

... AND THAT'S WHEN I
WOULD GRAB YOU AND
THROW YOU IN THE WATER.
THAT WAS GREAT.
THANKS, TREASURE.
WE'LL TRY TO LET
YOU KNOW BY
MONDAY.

THAT WAS AWFUL.
I LIKED HER READING.

BRADEN- WHOSE RAIN WAS BETTER - TREASURE MORSE OR MADISON VUONG?
OH, TREASURE, NO DOUBT.
WHAT?

MADISON WAS OVERACTING.
PLAY

SHE WAS QUEEN OF THE MERMAID PARADE THREE YEARS IN A ROW. SHE STARRED IN A TOOTHPASTE COMMERCIAL.
WHICH WOULD BE PERFECT IF OUR FILM WAS ABOUT CAVITIES.

RAIN'S FIGHT WITH DEREK IS THE CLIMAX OF THE WHOLE FILM. YOU CAN'T JUST HAVE SOMEONE DEADPAN THE LINES.

I WROTE THE LINES, SO I CAN DO WHATEVER I WANT.

I'M SORRY I HAD TO BABYSIT AND I DIDN'T SPEND AS MUCH TIME ON THE SCRIPT BUT I **DID** CONTRIBUTE.
I KNOW, AND I APPRECIATE THAT BUT-

I'M GOING HOME. BABYSITTING. BIG SHOCKER, I KNOW.
DANA!
JUST LET HER GO.

DON'T LET LILY GET UNDER YOUR SKIN.

SHE'S ON A POWER TRIP WITH THIS WHOLE DIRECTOR THING.
I KNOW.
PLAY

I JUST WISH SHE DIDN'T TAKE ME FOR GRANTED.
I DON'T TAKE YOU FOR GRANTED.

I, UM, I HAVE TO GO.

MRS. HOLMQUIST CALLED. SHE SAID YOU WERE ALMOST AN HOUR LATE TO GET JESSE TODAY.
I WAS STUDYING. I LOST TRACK OF TIME.

SHE SAID YOU'VE BEEN LATE ALL WEEK.
I'M DOING MY BEST, OKAY.

YOU REMEMBER WHAT IT'S LIKE TO BE THE LAST KID AT SCHOOL WAITING TO GET PICKED UP?

IT'S THE WORST FEELING IN THE ENTIRE WORLD.

WELL DON'T DO IT TO YOUR BROTHER, THEN.
YOU'RE DOING IT TO HIM. I NEVER ASKED FOR THIS RESPONSIBILITY.

KNOCK
KNOCK
KNOCK

DANA? WHAT ARE YOU DOING HERE?

I WANTED TO SEE YOU.
IT'S REALLY LATE.

CAN I COME IN?
YEAH, OF COURSE. COME AROUND FRONT. MY PARENTS ARE ASLEEP.

HOT ROD
HOT ROD
ARE YOU OKAY?
DO YOU LIKE ME?
I THOUGHT IT WAS OBVIOUS.
WHY?
BECAUSE I WAS FLIRTING WITH YOU?
HOTRODS

NO. I MEAN WHY DO YOU **LIKE** ME?

YOU HAVE UNUSUAL INTERESTS. YOU CARE ABOUT THINGS MOST PEOPLE DON'T EVEN THINK ABOUT.

HAVE YOU, UM, DONE THIS BEFORE?
YEAH, OF COURSE.

YOU NEVER TOLD ME.
I HAVE MY SECRETS.
HOT ROD

I WENT OVER TO BRADEN'S THAT NIGHT BECAUSE I WANTED TO BE THE CENTER OF SOMEONE'S ATTENTION. I TRUSTED BRADEN WITH MY LIFE, AND I KNEW HE CARED ABOUT ME. THE FUNNY THING WAS, THOUGH, THAT AFTER WE SLEPT TOGETHER, I FELT EVEN MORE ALONE THAN I DID BEFORE.

I'M REALLY SORRY ABOUT THE CASTING CALL. I WAS RUDE.
NAH, IT'S OKAY. I'VE JUST BEEN STRESSED OUT ABOUT MY COLLEGE APPLICATION.
WAITING'S THE WORST.

I, UM, ENDED UP OVER AT BRADEN'S.
OH MY GOD REALLY? HE **HAS** ALWAYS LIKED YOU. SO WHAT HAPPENED?

DING
THAT'S THE THING, I–

HEY Y'ALL!
WYE! HEY. HOW WAS WORK?
TASTY
CLOSE

HELLA SLOW. SHOCKINGLY, NO ONE WANTS TO GO SWIMMING IN A PILE OF ROTTING FISH.

I'M GONNA GO WASH MY HANDS. I'LL BE RIGHT BACK.

I THOUGHT YOU SAID YOU WANTED TO HANG OUT JUST THE TWO OF US.

IT TURNS OUT "NOSFERATU" IS LIKE WYE'S FAVORITE FILM AND THEY'VE NEVER SEEN IT ON THE BIG SCREEN.
SORRY I SPACED ON THAT.
I REALLY DIDN'T THINK YOU'D MIND.

YOU KNOW, I DIDN'T SLEEP TOO WELL LAST NIGHT AND I HAVE A LOT OF HOMEWORK TO DO.
NO WORRIES.
I MIGHT BAIL ON THE MATINÉE.

ARE YOU SURE?
YEAH. I'LL SEE YOU AROUND.
SAY BYE TO WYE FOR ME.

CHAPTER SIX

CITY HAL
ACT
CLIMATE RALLY
CITY HALL
ONLY ONE EARTH

ACTION NOW!

WE'RE HERE TODAY WITH A VERY SPECIFIC GOAL.

WE DEMAND MAYOR HARGRAVE ENROLL BOCA BELLA IN THE CITIES FOR CLIMATE PROTECTION INITIATIVE, WHICH LAYS OUT STEPS WE CAN TAKE TO CURB THE DISASTROUS EFFECTS OF OCEAN WARMING..

IF WE DON'T ACT IMMEDIATELY, FUTURE GENERATIONS WILL WONDER WHY WE STOOD BY AND DID NOTHING.
NOW

WELL I'M HERE TO DO SOMETHING. SAY IT WITH ME! WHAT DO WE WANT? CLIMATE ACTION! WHEN DO WE WANT IT? NOW!
WHAT DO WE WANT? CLIMATE ACTION! WHEN DO WE WANT IT? NOW! WHAT DO WE WANT? CLIMATE ACTION! WHEN DO WE WANT IT? NOW!

DAPHNE!
DANA! I'M SURPRISED TO SEE YOU.

WHAT ARE YOU DOING?
HORSE CRAZY

WE'RE STAGING A DIE-IN.

YOU'RE A FILMMAKER.

YOU UNDERSTAND THE POWER OF THE SPECTACLE.
HORSE CRAZ

EVERYONE CLEAR OUT
BPD

YOU'RE VIOLATING CITY FIRE CODES.

AS YOU SEE, OFFICER, I CAN'T DO THAT.
THEN I HAVE TO ARREST YOU.

YOU DON'T HAVE TO DO ANYTHING. EVERY ONE OF YOUR ACTIONS IS A CHOICE.

DAPHNE!

SNIP

OH GOOD. THE CAMERAS HAVE ARRIVED.
POLICE

BOCA BELLA SHERIFF
POLICE

I'M HERE FOR DAPHNE OCEAN. SHE'S ONE OF THE CLIMATE PROTESTERS.

YOU MEAN DIANE DIRUSSO? WE'RE HOLDING HER OVERNIGHT. IF SHE POSTS BAIL, YOU CAN PICK HER UP IN THE MORNING.

A CLIMATE PROTEST AT CITY HALL TURNED VIOLENT TODAY WHEN PROTESTERS CLASHED WITH POLICE.

I TOLD YOU THAT WOMAN WAS A NUTCASE.

CAN I BORROW THE CAR TOMORROW?
WHAT FOR?
I NEED TO PICK UP SOME PROPS.
FINE, BUT I NEED IT BACK BY FIVE.

SO YOUR NAME'S DIANE?
GOSH, NO ONE'S CALLED ME THAT IN A LONG TIME.

MY MOM THINKS YOU'RE A WITCH AND YOU HEXED CITY HALL. SHE THINKS YOU'RE DANGEROUS.

NO, NO HEXES. THEY HAVE A HABIT OF BACKFIRING.

BUT YOU'RE NOT A **REAL** WITCH. I MEAN, MAGIC ISN'T REAL.
IF YOU SET A GOAL, AND FOCUS YOUR ENERGY ON IT, ARE YOU MORE LIKELY TO ACHIEVE THAT GOAL?
YEAH, I GUESS SO.

WELL, I WORK WITH THE FOUR ELEMENTS TO CREATE AND CHANNEL ENERGY. YOU'RE CONSTANTLY CREATING ENERGY, YOU JUST HAVEN'T LEARNED TO CHANNEL IT YET.

WILL YOU SHOW ME?

JO ONCE TOLD ME "IF IT SEEMS TOO GOOD TO BE TRUE, IT PROBABLY IS." SHE WAS REFERRING TO THE GUY WHO SELLS FAKE ROLEXES IN THE COST-LOW PARKING LOT, BUT IT HOLDS TRUE IN MY EXPERIENCE. SO I WAS FEELING PRETTY SKEPTICAL OF DAPHNE'S MAGICAL ABILITIES.
EACH ONE OF THE OBJECTS ON THIS ALTAR REPRESENTS ONE OF THE FOUR ELEMENTS.

THAT'S BEAUTIFUL.
I'M A WATER WITCH, AND THE CHALICE REPRESENTS WATER. MY HUSBAND, ARTHUR, WAS A POTTER. HE MADE IT ESPECIALLY FOR ME.
HORSECRAZY

SET AN INTENTION. IT NEEDS TO BE SOMETHING SPECIFIC AND ATTAINABLE. YOU WILL SPEND FIVE MINUTES, TWICE A DAY, VISUALIZING THIS GOAL.

I WANT TO GET INTO NYU

NOW DON'T SHOW ME. JUST FOLD THE SLIP OF PAPER IN HALF AND PUT IT IN THE CAULDRON.

FWOOSH

SHE THREW A MATCH INTO THE CAULDRON AND THE FLAME TURNED BRIGHT BLUE.

COPPER CHLORIDE, PROBABLY. THAT'S HOW THEY COLOR FIREWORKS.
STAGE MAGICIANS USE IT ALL THE TIME. WHAT DID YOU WISH FOR?

TO GET INTO NYU, OBVIOUSLY.
DRESSES
NO RETURNS

YOU'LL BE ACCEPTED FOR SURE, BUT WITH MY SAT SCORES, I'M GONNA NEED MAGIC.
BE CAREFUL OR YOU'RE GOING TO END UP YELLING INTO A MEGAPHONE ON A STREET CORNER SOMEWHERE.
CROC&ROLL

SHE'S NOT CRAZY.
SHOUTING ON STREET CORNERS IS THE DEFINITION OF CRAZY.

AT LEAST SHE CARES ABOUT SOMETHING.
COME ON Y'ALL. WE'D BETTER GET GOING IF WE'RE GOING TO MEET TREASURE.

THRIFT MART

TO MAKE A LATEX MASK, FIRST YOU HAVE TO CAST YOUR ACTOR'S FACE. STEP ONE: WAX YOUR ACTOR'S EYEBROWS SO THE ALGINATE DOESN'T RIP THEM OFF.

STEP TWO: MIX YOUR ALGINATE WITH REALLY COLD WATER. I USE DENTAL ALGINATE, THE STUFF THAT DENTISTS USE TO CAST FALSE TEETH. YOU HAVE TO WORK FAST, BEFORE IT STARTS TO SET.

STEP THREE: SLATHER THE GOO ALL OVER YOUR ACTOR'S FACE. PRESS HARD AGAINST THEIR SKIN TO GET RID OF AIR BUBBLES.

HOLD STILL AND CLOSE YOUR EYES.
OH NO. YOU ARE **NOT** COVERING MY EYES.

I HAVE TO OR THE MOLD WON'T BE STABLE. I HAVE TO COVER YOUR MOUTH TOO, BUT I'M GOING TO LEAVE NOSE HOLES SO YOU CAN BREATHE.

THIS IS REALLY FREAKING ME OUT.

YOU HOLD YOUR BREATH UNDERWATER.
I'M FEELING REALLY CLAUSTROPHOBIC...

IT ONLY TAKES FIFTEEN MINUTES. I PROMISE IT WON'T BE THAT BAD.

LIKE I'M BEING BURIED ALIVE!

DANA-LET'S JUST FORGET ABOUT IT. MAYBE WE DON'T NEED A FULL MASK. IT MIGHT BE COOL IF SHE LOOKED MOSTLY HUMAN WITH JUST SOME GILLS ON HER NECK OR SOMETHING.
I WAS REALLY LOOKING FORWARD TO A FULL FACIAL SCULPT. IT'S LIKE, NOW I'M DOING ALMOST NOTHING ON THIS PROJECT.

CHAPTER SEVEN

AFTER THE MASK FIASCO, I WENT WHERE I ALWAYS GO WHEN I NEED SOME PERSPECTIVE: OCEANVIEW CEMETERY.

DANA. HOW ARE YOU?

HAVING A PICNIC?
LOCATION SCOUTING. YOU OKAY?

WHEN YOU WERE WORKING ON YOUR FILMS, DID YOU EVER FIGHT WITH YOUR CREW?
I HAVE HORROR STORIES. EVERYONE IN THE INDUSTRY DOES.

WAS THERE EVER A TIME WHEN YOU WANTED TO QUIT?

I HAD A FRIEND, A REALLY GREAT CINEMATOGRAPHER, WHO I HIRED TO WORK ON "CROSSROADS SONG."

IT'S SET IN MISSISSIPPI, MOSTLY IMPROVISED, WITH AN ALL-BLACK CAST.

WELL, THIS GUY HAD NEVER HAD TO CAPTURE SUCH A WIDE RANGE OF SKIN TONES BEFORE, AND HE DIDN'T UNDERSTAND HOW TO CORRECTLY LIGHT THE DARK-SKINNED ACTORS.

WHAT DID YOU DO?

I TRIED GIVING CONSTRUCTIVE CRITICISM, BUT HE TOOK IT AS A PERSONAL ATTACK. FINALLY, I HAD TO LET HIM GO.

YOU FIRED HIM?
YES, AND WE HAVEN'T SPOKEN SINCE. THIS WAS THE MAN I BROUGHT TO MY SISTER'S WEDDING.

WOW.
I HAD A REALLY HARD TIME WITH LINDA WARD, THE STAR OF "VOIDCRAWLERS".
MONROE

I WANTED A DIFFERENT ACTRESS FOR THE ROLE. THE PRODUCERS INSISTED ON LINDA BECAUSE SHE HAD NAME RECOGNITION. IT'S ALL ABOUT MONEY FOR THEM.

IS THAT WHY YOU LEFT HOLLY-WOOD?
MY MOM HAS ALZHEIMER'S. SHE WAS DIAGNOSED LAST SPRING. I CAME BACK TO TAKE CARE OF HER.

SO YOU'RE DONE MAKING MOVIES?

YOU KIDDING? IN THE PAST YEAR, I'VE WRITTEN ONE SCRIPT AND STARTED CROWDFUNDING ANOTHER. ONCE YOU'VE GOT THE BUG, IT'S NOT EASY TO STOP.

I WAS STILL DISAPPOINTED AFTER MY CONVERSATION WITH JEANINE, BUT ACCORDING TO HER, DISAPPOINTMENT IS A MAJOR PART OF FILMMAKING.

SO I WENT BACK TO WORK.
PLACES! WE'VE GOT TO FINISH BLOCKING AND START SHOOTING ASAP IF WE WANT TO BE EDITING BY APRIL. WHEN I SAY ACTION, WE'LL DO A RUN-THROUGH.

DANA- WILL YOU GO IN THE KITCHEN AND GRAB ME A SODA?
SSSURE.

HISSSSS

HISSS

DAPHNE? ARE YOU OKAY?
WHAT? OH YES. JUST RESTING MY EYES.

YOU WEREN'T... DOING ANYTHING TO THAT GLASS OF WATER?

I HEARD LAUGHTER IN THE LIVING ROOM AND IT BROUGHT ME BACK TO MY HIGH SCHOOL DAYS. IT'S FUN HAVING YOUNG PEOPLE IN THE HOUSE.
DAPHNE, WHY DIDN'T YOU AND ARTHUR EVER HAVE KIDS?

HAH. WE WERE SO HAPPY TOGETHER, WE DIDN'T NEED ANYONE ELSE. BY THE TIME WE CONSIDERED IT, WE FOUND OUR CHANCE HAD PASSED.
DO YOU REGRET IT?

MY MOTHER HAD VERY SPECIFIC IDEAS ABOUT HOW WOMEN SHOULD THINK AND ACT. IN MY TEENS, MY MAIN AMBITION WAS TO BE HER EXACT OPPOSITE.

DO YOU STILL TALK TO HER?

SHE PASSED AWAY MANY YEARS AGO, AND WE FOUGHT LIKE WET CATS RIGHT UP UNTIL THE END. THE ONE TRAIT WE SHARED WAS EXTREME STUBBORNNESS.

MARCH
MO TUE WE TH FR SA SUN
1 2 3 4 5 6 7
8 9 10 11 12 13 14
15 16 17 18 19 20 21

I AM TELLING YOU, THE WATER IN THAT GLASS WAS BOILING.
OKAY, PROFESSOR. WHAT IS IT?
THERE'S GOT TO BE A RATIONAL EXPLANATION.

THE LOWER THE ATMOSPHERIC PRESSURE, THE LOWER THE BOILING POINT OF WATER. THAT'S WHY ASTRONAUTS WEAR PRESSURIZED SUITS. OTHERWISE, THEIR BLOOD WOULD LITERALLY BOIL.

IF THE PRESSURE HAD BEEN LOW ENOUGH TO BOIL WATER, MY BLOOD WOULD HAVE ALSO BOILED, WHICH I'M PRETTY SURE I WOULD HAVE NOTICED.

MAYBE YOU SAW A REFLECTION IN THE GLASS.
I SWEAR TO GOD, THE WATER WAS BOILING.

I BELIEVE YOU.

WORREL'S
MARINA

KNOTTY BOY

DEREK!
DERRRRREEEEKK

RAIN! RAIN! I HEAR YOU. I'M COMING!
KNOTT BOY

SPLASH
TTY BOY

RAIN! I LOVE YOU!

THIS IS WHEN I'M SUPPOSED TO BITE HIM, RIGHT? OH MY GOD, I CAN'T DO THIS.

AHAHAHAHA
HEHEHE
HAHAHA

CUT! CUT GODDAMMIT.

I'VE GOT SWIM PRACTICE. I'VE GOTTA GO.
IT'S TOO DARK TO KEEP SHOOTING ANYWAY. WE'LL HAVE TO TRY AGAIN LATER. DANA—GET SOME STILL SHOTS OF THE ACTORS FOR CONTINUITY.
OTTY BO

COME IN. YOU'RE SOAKED! HOW WAS THE SHOOT?

WE DIDN'T GET THE FOOTAGE WE WANTED. WE'LL HAVE TO TRY AGAIN AFTER SPRING BREAK.

WAIT. WHY NOT DURING SPRING BREAK?
WE'RE GOING TO SAVANNAH.

WHO'S GOING TO SAVANNAH?
ME AND LILY. SHE DIDN'T TELL YOU?
NO, SHE MUST HAVE FORGOT TO MENTION IT.

I APPLIED TO THE SAVANNAH COLLEGE OF ART & DESIGN. WYE'S TOURING THE CAMPUS WITH ME.

DID YOU KNOW ABOUT THIS, BRADEN?

OH MY GOD, YOU DID!

IT SOUNDS LIKE A GREAT OPPORTUNITY.
I THOUGHT YOU WERE ON MY SIDE.

I DIDN'T KNOW THERE WERE SIDES.

WHY DIDN'T YOU TELL ME?
YOU'VE BEEN ACTING REALLY PISSY LATELY. I KNEW YOU'D MAKE IT A BIG DEAL.

WE WERE SUPPOSED TO GO TO NEW YORK TOGETHER. WE'VE BEEN PLANNING IT SINCE SIXTH GRADE. NOW YOU'RE, WHAT, BACKING OUT? WHAT AM I SUPPOSED TO DO?

FRIENDSHIPS EVOLVE IN UNPREDICTABLE WAYS. SOMETIMES TWO PLANTS POTTED IN THE SAME SOIL NEED A LITTLE SPACE TO GROW.

WOW, THAT'S DEEP, **DIANE!** YOU ARE SUCH A FAKE. YOU USE A FAKE NAME, YOU PRETEND YOU HAVE MAGIC POWERS, YOU ACT LIKE YOU KNOW THE SECRET TO THE UNIVERSE, BUT JO'S RIGHT. YOU'RE JUST A LONELY WINGNUT.

DANA, I'M SORRY I HURT YOUR FEELINGS—
FORGET IT LILY. YOU'RE NOTHING TO ME. YOU CAN ALL GO TO HELL.

MOST AMERICAN FILMS HAVE THREE ACTS: SETUP, CONFRONTATION, AND RESOLUTION. MY FIGHT WITH LILY WAS BAD, BUT I KNEW FROM STUDYING SCREENWRITING THAT IN THE THIRD ACT, THINGS USUALLY GET A WHOLE LOT WORSE BEFORE THEY GET BETTER.

DANA! COME HELP ME CARRY THESE SUITCASES TO THE CAR.
KNOCK KNOCK

I THOUGHT YOU WERE LEAVING TOMORROW AFTERNOON.

I'M WORKING A MORNING SHIFT. I NEED EVERYTHING PACKED SO I CAN PICK JESSE UP AFTER SCHOOL AND GO STRAIGHT TO THE MARINA.

YOU CAN STILL COME IF YOU WANT. ALL YOU HAVE TO DO IS APOLOGIZE.
BIOHAZARD

NO THANKS. I'M GOOD.

BUZZ

BRADEN
TODAY 5 PM
HOW R U?
BRADEN IS TYPING

DING
BRADEN
HOW R U?
SAY SOMETHING PLEASE.

SPRING
BREAK

3/9

3/10

3/11

3/12

3/13
PIZZA
PIZZA

LOOKS LIKE WE'RE OUT OF FOOD, RIGEL.

MA

COST-LOW
GROCERY

PIZZA
CAT
PEANU
WHEAT CRACKERS

SUPER SALE
BAGGED ICE $5

DING DING
SPRING BREAK EXPRESS

HEY! WATCH WHERE YOU'RE GOING!

DRIVE OFF A CLIFF, ASSHOLE.

HEY, LOVELY- LONG TIME NO SEE.

COME IN AND GET COMFY. THERE'S PLENTY OF BEER IN THE FRIDGE.

SIGH.
ALRIGHT, DYLAN.
SERIOUSLY?

IT'S BEEN A REALLY BAD WEEK.

KITCHEN'S BACK AND TO YOUR RIGHT.

YEAH!
EEK
WOOO
HAHAHAHA

BOOM♪
BOOM♪
BOOM♪

BOOM
BOOM
BOOM♪

BOOM BOOM
BOOM

DANA! WAIT!

CAT
CAT
CAT

IT WAS LIKE THAT EPISODE OF "WARP WIZARDS" WHERE THE FISHERMAN WISHED TO BE RICH, SO THE EVIL GENIE KILLED THE FISHERMAN'S WIFE AND GAVE HIM THE LIFE INSURANCE MONEY. I THOUGHT I WANTED MY FRIENDS TO LEAVE ME ALONE, BUT ONCE I'D GOTTEN MY WISH, I WAS MISERABLE.

DANA! WHAT ON EARTH? THIS IS DISGUSTING.
LOOKS LIKE A CATEGORY 2 CAME THROUGH HERE.
PIZZA

HEY LITTLE BROTHER, YOU GET A BIT SUNBURNED?

HIS SUPPOSEDLY WATERPROOF SUNSCREEN CAME OFF IN THE SWIMMING POOL.
BY THE TIME WE REALIZED, HE WAS COOKED LIKE A ROTISSERIE CHICKEN.

WORST TRIP EVER.

THIS CAME IN THE MAIL FOR YOU.
IT'S FROM NYU.
HOME SWEET

AREN'T YOU GOING TO OPEN IT?

I DON'T NEED TO.
WHAT DO YOU MEAN?
PIZZA

THIS ENVELOPE IS THIN. IF I'D BEEN ACCEPTED, IT'D BE FAT. THERE'D BE PAMPHLETS INSIDE ABOUT HOW TO REGISTER FOR CLASSES AND SIGN UP FOR A MEAL PLAN AND STUFF.

THIS ENVELOPE IS THIN BECAUSE THERE'S NOTHING INSIDE BUT A REJECTION LETTER.

COME ON, DANA, YOU DON'T KNOW THAT. JUST GO AHEAD AND OPEN IT.
IF YOU'RE SO SURE, WHY DON'T YOU OPEN IT?

RIP

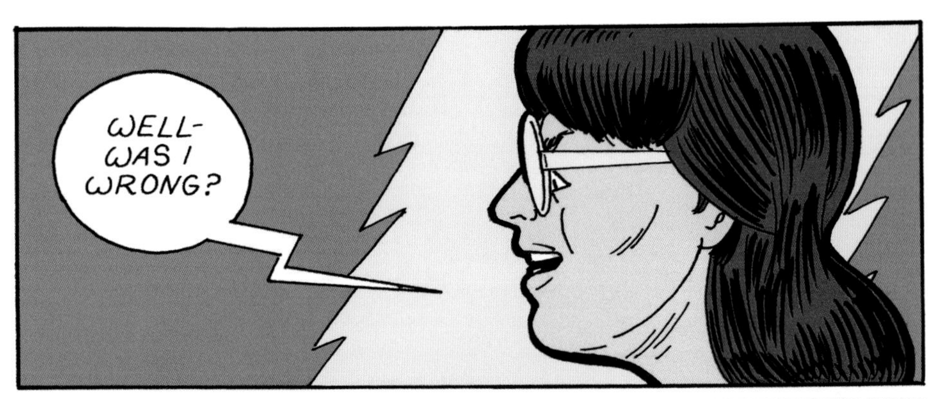
WELL-
WAS I
WRONG?

I DIDN'T
THINK SO!
PIZZA

MY ACCEPTANCE LETTER FROM NYU WAS SUPPOSED TO SHOW MY CLASSMATES THAT I WAS AN ECCENTRIC GENIUS AND NOT THE SAD SCREW-UP THEY'D ALWAYS THOUGHT I WAS. AND NOW I WASN'T EVEN GOING TO GRADUATE HIGH SCHOOL.
HEY.
GO AWAY.

I'M SORRY ABOUT NYU.
IT'S NOT JUST THAT. I'M WORRIED ABOUT MY FILM CLASS.
I THOUGHT YOU LOVED THAT CLASS.

I GOT IN A BIG FIGHT WITH LILY AND I DITCHED OUR FINAL PROJECT. IF I DON'T TURN IN SOMETHING, I COULD BE EXPELLED.

I'M SURE IF YOU APOLOGIZE, LILY'LL TAKE YOU BACK.
I DON'T WANT HER TO TAKE ME BACK. I CAN DO THIS ON MY OWN.

DO YOU REMEMBER WHEN YOU WERE FIVE AND YOU CAUGHT THAT GROUPER AT WORREL'S MARINA?
YES. YOU'VE TOLD ME THAT STORY A MILLION TIMES.

IT WAS HUGE, A 10-POUNDER. ALL THE OTHER KIDS ON THE DOCK WERE SHOUTING AND CHEERING, BUT YOU BAWLED YOUR EYES OUT. YOU CRIED SO HARD, YOU BEGGED ME TO THROW IT BACK.

WHAT DOES THAT HAVE TO DO WITH ANYTHING?
I KNEW THE WORLD WAS GOING TO BE HARD ON YOU. I FIGURED IF I WAS HARD ON YOU TOO, IT MIGHT TOUGHEN YOU UP.

I HATED YOU FOR IT.
BUT YOU GOT TOUGH.

MAYBE I GOT TOO TOUGH.

CHAPTER EIGHT

WHY DIDN'T YOU TELL ME ABOUT LILY AND WYE'S ROAD TRIP?
I WAS WAITING FOR ONE OF THEM TO TELL YOU. IT SEEMED LIKE NONE OF MY BUSINESS.

MY BEST FRIEND BASICALLY GHOSTED ME. IT REALLY, REALLY HURT.
I KNOW HOW IT FEELS. **TRUST ME**.

BRADEN, I-
I REALLY LIKED YOU. I THOUGHT YOU FELT THE SAME WAY. AND THEN YOU DITCHED ME AND WOULDN'T RETURN MY TEXTS.

I'M SORRY YOU SAW ME WITH TREASURE, BUT WE DIDN'T DO ANYTHING WRONG.
DO YOU LIKE HER?

I LIKE HANGING OUT WITH HER. I THINK SHE CARES ABOUT ME.
I CARE ABOUT YOU.
BUT YOU DON'T LIKE ME.

NOT LIKE THAT. BUT I THOUGHT I MIGHT.
WHAT YOU DID WAS REALLY SELFISH.

I CAN BE BETTER. I WANT TO BE A GOOD FRIEND.
THEN BE A GOOD FRIEND, DANA. NO ONE'S STOPPING YOU.

DANA, I'M ITCHY.
GO PUT ON SOME LOTION, KIDDO.
I ALREADY DID.

THEN GO PUT ON SOME MORE.
CLICK

WE'RE FILMING LIVE OUTSIDE CITY HALL TONIGHT, WHERE A SMALL GROUP OF ACTIVISTS HAS GATHERED, BLOCKING THE INTERSECTION AT SPRUCE STREET.
ACT!

THE CITY COUNCIL VOTED TODAY ON A CLIMATE INITIATIVE THAT WOULD HAVE SIGNIFICANTLY REDUCED CARBON EMISSIONS IN BOCA BELLA.
HONK
HONK
HONK
HALL
ACT NOW

SOLUTIONS NOT POLLUTION
NO NATURE NO FUTURE
THE COUNCIL REJECTED THE INITIATIVE 4-2.

HEY, JESS, PUT ON A SHIRT TOO. I'M TAKING YOU TO MRS. AVILA'S.

HOOONK

HONK HONK

NO NATURE NO FUTURE
DANA, GOOD TO SEE YOU.

WHAT I SAID WAS AWFUL.

YES IT WAS. HERE. TAKE MY SIGN.
YOU'RE NOT STILL MAD AT ME?
NO NATURE NO FUTURE

I'M SIXTY-FIVE. I DON'T HAVE THE ENERGY TO HOLD A GRUDGE.

DAPHNE, HAVE THERE EVER BEEN TIMES WHERE YOU SET AN INTENTION AND IT DIDN'T WORK OUT?
NO NATURE NO FUTURE

IF MAGIC WAS INFALLIBLE, DO YOU THINK I'D STILL BE OUT HERE PROTESTING?
NO NATURE NO FUTURE

WHAT WILL YOU DO NOW THAT YOU LOST THE VOTE?

WE'LL KEEP FIGHTING. WE'VE BEEN FUNDRAISING ONLINE AND WE'RE PLANNING A BIG EARTH DAY ACTION.
LIKE THE DIE-IN?
NO NATURE NO FUTURE

WE HAVEN'T DECIDED. IT NEEDS TO BE BIGGER. LOUDER...
... IMPOSSIBLE TO IGNORE? I THINK I MIGHT HAVE AN IDEA.

THERE'S A COMMITTEE MEETING ON SUNDAY. WHY DON'T YOU COME AND SHARE IT WITH THE GROUP?
NO NATURE NO FUTURE

THE ANCHORWATCH CHAPTER IN ZAMBIA IS HOLDING A MOCK FUNERAL FOR MOTHER EARTH. THE CHAPTER IN VIENNA IS BLOCKING TRAFFIC ON THE KARLSPLATZ.

DOES ANYONE HAVE SUGGESTIONS FOR OUR OWN EARTH DAY ACTION?

WHAT IF WE PUT ON ZOMBIE MAKEUP AND CRASHED THE MERMAID PARADE?
IT DOESN'T FALL ON EARTH DAY, BUT IT IS IN APRIL, AND THE WHOLE TOWN WILL BE THERE.

I THINK IT'S IMPORTANT WE STICK WITH EARTH DAY, IN SOLIDARITY.
DISRUPTING THE MERMAID PARADE WOULD SEND A MESSAGE.

WHAT KIND OF MESSAGE? I'M NOT SURE SHOUTING DOWN A PARADE IS THE RIGHT WAY TO GET ATTENTION.
MARINE MAMMALS ARE FACING EXTINCTION AND YOU'RE WORRIED ABOUT POLITENESS?

GOALS
OBJECTIVES
TACTICS
#1DAD
WHY DON'T WE PUT IT TO A VOTE? SHOW OF HANDS, WHO SUPPORTS DISRUPTING THE MERMAID PARADE?

8 TO 4. THE AYES HAVE IT.

AFTER THAT, THINGS MOVED REALLY FAST. THE BOAT HANGAR WAS BUSY NIGHT AND DAY. A RADICAL PUPPET THEATER CAME FROM ENGLEWOOD, ABOUT HALF AN HOUR AWAY. THEY BROUGHT A BUNCH OF AMAZING PROPS AND AN... INTERESTING VOLUNTEER.

A HOT OLDER BOY WHO DRANK COFFEE AFTER DARK AND KNEW TRAGIC EDWARDIAN AUTHOR FACTS? MY HEART WAS EXPLODING, BUT NOT FROM A WOODEN STAKE.

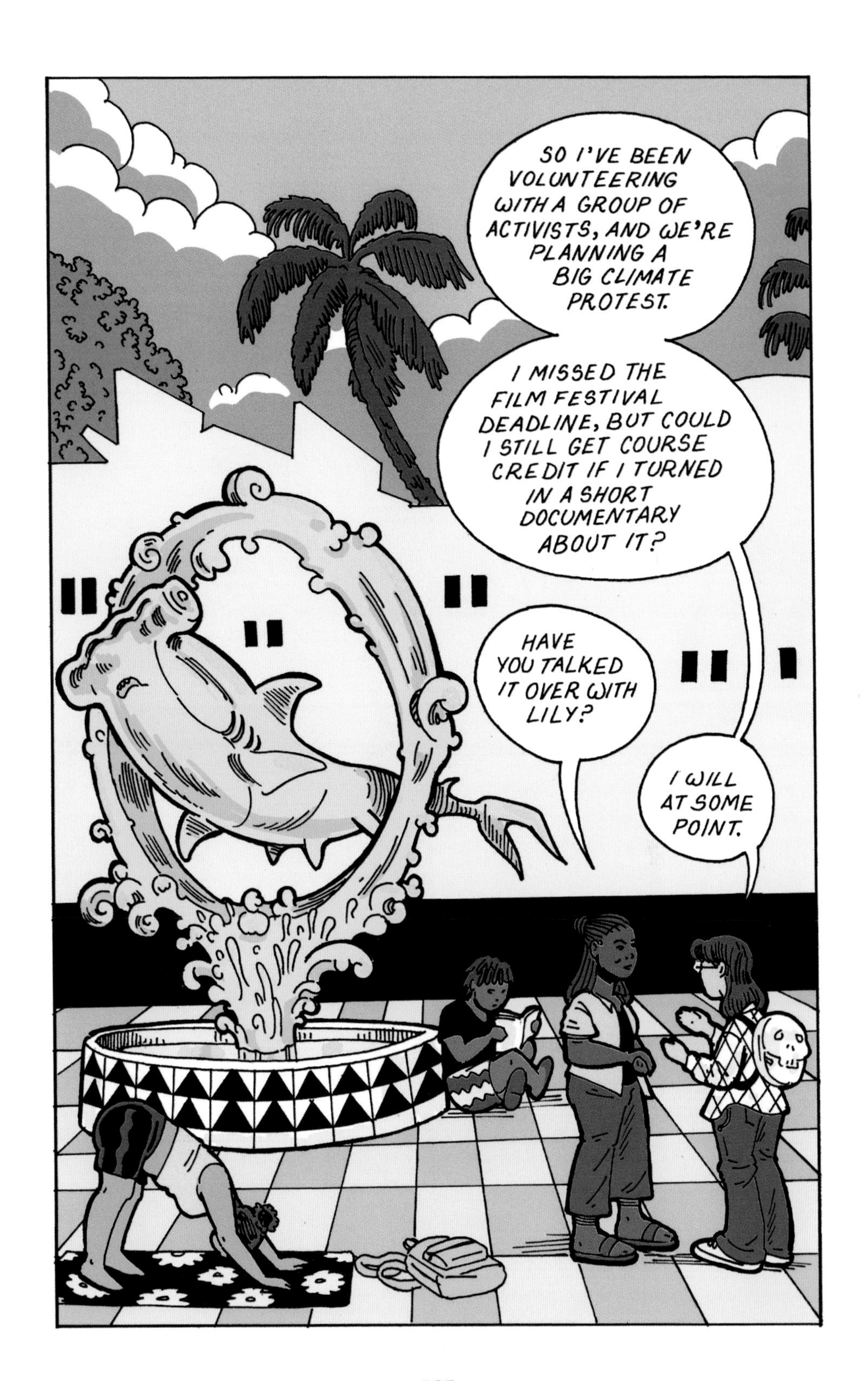
SO I'VE BEEN VOLUNTEERING WITH A GROUP OF ACTIVISTS, AND WE'RE PLANNING A BIG CLIMATE PROTEST.
I MISSED THE FILM FESTIVAL DEADLINE, BUT COULD I STILL GET COURSE CREDIT IF I TURNED IN A SHORT DOCUMENTARY ABOUT IT?
HAVE YOU TALKED IT OVER WITH LILY?
I WILL AT SOME POINT.

YOU'RE HEADING OFF TO SCHOOL SOON. DON'T LET BAD BLOOD RUIN YOUR LAST MONTHS TOGETHER.

LILY'S GOING TO SCHOOL. I'M NOT. I DIDN'T GET INTO NYU.

SURELY YOU APPLIED TO SOME SAFETY SCHOOLS?
NO.

OH. WELL, YOU CAN ALWAYS TAKE A GAP YEAR.

YOU DON'T THINK I'VE SCREWED UP MY FUTURE FOREVER?

THE ONLY WAY TO SCREW UP YOUR FUTURE IS TO FALL FOR THE LIE THAT SUCCESS ONLY MEANS ONE THING.
I'VE ONLY EVER WANTED ONE THING.

ALL THE MORE REASON TO GO OUT AND LIVE SOME LIFE.

I WENT TO ACCRA, GHANA, TO VISIT AN EX, DISCOVERED FANTASY COFFINS- COMPLETELY BY ACCIDENT- AND ENDED UP FILMING A SHORT ABOUT THE ARTISTS WHO CARVE THEM.

THAT SHORT GOT ME INTO FILM SCHOOL.
WHAT ARE FANTASY COFFINS?
SHARKS ATTACK!

PAINTED CASKETS IN THE SHAPE OF ANIMALS, VEHICLES, EVEN SNEAKERS...

THEY'RE MEANT TO HONOR THE DECEASED BY REPRESENTING A LIFE GOAL OR AN ASPECT OF THEIR PERSONALITY.
WHAT WOULD YOUR FANTASY COFFIN BE?

A SONY PDF 150 VIDEO CAMERA. CHEAP, LIGHTWEIGHT, 40-MINUTE TAKES, AUTOMATIC FOCUS. CAN YOU TELL I'VE THOUGHT ABOUT THIS?

HOW ABOUT YOU?
I-I'M NOT SURE.
FIGURE IT OUT. YOU'VE GOT PLENTY OF TIME.

LILY, WYE, HI!

IT'S OKAY, DANA. WE WERE JUST LEAVING.

WAIT. JUST LISTEN FOR A MINUTE?

SAY WHAT YOU NEED TO SAY. WE'RE SHOOTING IN HALF AN HOUR.

GROWING UP, I WAS ALWAYS HAPPY TO BE YOUR SIDEKICK.

WHEN YOU STARTED SEEING WYE, I REALIZED I MIGHT HAVE TO MAKE MY OWN DECISIONS ABOUT WHERE TO LIVE AND WORK AND STUDY... AND IT WAS TERRIFYING.
$1.50
THE BOCA BELLA HERALD
RED TIDE

IF I'M SUCH A CONTROL FREAK, WHY DID YOU EVER HANG OUT WITH ME?

YOU'RE NOT A CONTROL FREAK. YOUR PERSONALITY'S JUST... BIGGER THAN MINE. YOU ALWAYS HAD STRONG OPINIONS, SO I DID WHATEVER YOU WANTED TO DO.

AND IT WORKED FOR A REALLY LONG TIME. UNTIL IT DIDN'T.

WHAT YOU DID TO BRADEN WAS REALLY MESSED UP, YOU KNOW.
I TRIED TO TALK TO YOU ABOUT HIM, BUT YOU WERE DISTRACTED. NO OFFENSE, WYE.

I GOT INTO COLLEGE IN SAVANNAH. WE'RE GOING TOGETHER IN THE FALL.

THAT'S GREAT! I'M SO HAPPY FOR YOU.
PAWN

I **WAS** HAPPY FOR THEM. I REALLY AND TRULY WAS. THAT DIDN'T MEAN I WASN'T STILL A LITTLE JEALOUS OF THEIR FAIRY-TALE ROMANCE, BUT THIS TIME, I WASN'T GOING TO LET IT POISON ME. BESIDES, I HAD A DOCUMENTARY TO FILM.

SOLAR POWER
FREE WHEEL PUPPET THEATER

HIGHER! YOU'VE GOT TO HOLD THE HEAD UP HIGHER.
MOVE IT TO THE LEFT! THE LEFT!

NOW THERE'S TOO MUCH WEIGHT ON MY SIDE!

CRASH

IT'S OKAY. WE CAN GLUE IT BACK ON.

THIS IS WHAT WE'LL BE USING FOR THE FAKE WOUNDS. IT'S CALLED A/B SILICONE.
A

MIX EQUAL PARTS OF SOLUTIONS A AND B, AND THE SILICONE STARTS TO CURE.

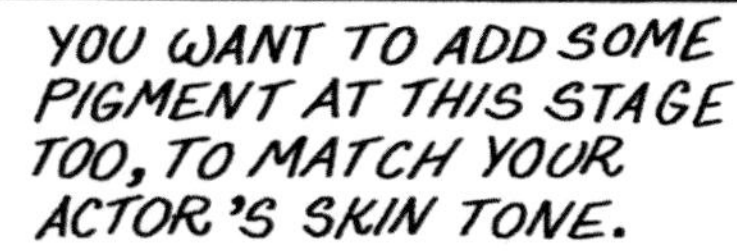
YOU WANT TO ADD SOME PIGMENT AT THIS STAGE TOO, TO MATCH YOUR ACTOR'S SKIN TONE.

ONCE IT'S MIXED, YOU'VE GOT A COUPLE MINUTES BEFORE THE SILICONE STARTS TO HARDEN.

ALCOHOL MAKES IT EASIER TO APPLY.

PUT A DECENT-SIZED GLOB ON YOUR ACTOR'S HEAD.

THEN SMOOTH IT OUT WITH A FAN BRUSH.

NOW, USE THE PALETTE KNIFE TO CARVE YOUR WOUND.

THE SILICONE WILL BE SHINY. DUST IT WITH POWDERED SUGAR TO GIVE IT TEXTURE.

NOW IT'S TIME TO PAINT.

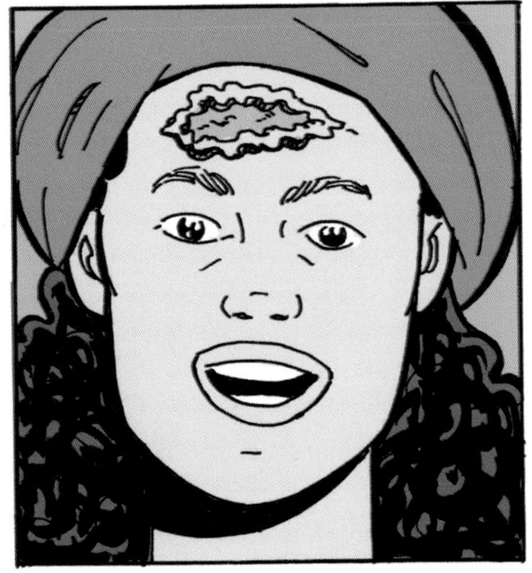

THAT IS DISGUSTING.
I HAVEN'T EVEN ADDED THE BLOOD YET.

NOW, I'LL SET UP SUPPLY STATIONS AROUND THE HANGAR.

ON PARADE DAY, EVERYONE CAN COME IN, APPLY EACH OTHER'S WOUNDS, AND BE GOOD TO GO.

FANTASTIC, DANA, THANK YOU. IS THAT ALL?
ONE MORE THING.

AT THE PARADE KICKOFF, THE MAYOR GETS UP ON A FLOAT TO CROWN THE MERMAID QUEEN. USUALLY SHE'S A VALEDICTORIAN OR THE OWNER OF A LOCAL BUSINESS.
WHAT IF WE DRESS SOMEONE AS A ZOMBIE QUEEN AND SEND **HER** UP TO ACCEPT THE AWARD?

SECURITY WOULD PULL HER OFFSTAGE BEFORE SHE COULD EVEN SPEAK.
IT'S WORTH A SHOT. DISRUPTING THE MAYOR'S SPEECH WOULD MEAN GUARANTEED PRESS COVERAGE.

DAPHNE, YOU COULD DO IT.

THAT'S FLATTERING, BUT I NOMINATE YOU.

IF YOU NEED A FAKE DECAYING EYEBALL OR A NASTY CHEST WOUND, I'M YOUR GIRL. BUT GETTING UP IN FRONT OF A WHOLE PARADE? THE THOUGHT MADE MY SKIN CRAWL. EVEN SO, I AGREED. I WANTED TO BE AS BRAVE AS MY FRIENDS THOUGHT I WAS.

FOR A WEEK STRAIGHT, I SPENT EVERY FREE MINUTE AT THE MARINA. ON NIGHTS WHEN JO HAD TO WORK, I BROUGHT JESSE. IT WAS CHAOTIC AND OVERWHELMING, AND THERE WERE TIMES WHEN IT SEEMED IMPOSSIBLE, BUT ON THE DAY OF THE MARCH, EVERYTHING CAME INTO FOCUS.

THEY'RE CROWNING THE MERMAID QUEEN BY THE BOARDWALK AT NOON. WE'LL CUT THROUGH COQUINA PARK TO INTERCEPT THEM.
WIND POWER NOW!
ONLY ONE EARTH

MEDICS, GRAB A FIRST-AID KIT.
AND DON'T FORGET TO STAY HYDRATED.

CLIMATE ACTION NOW

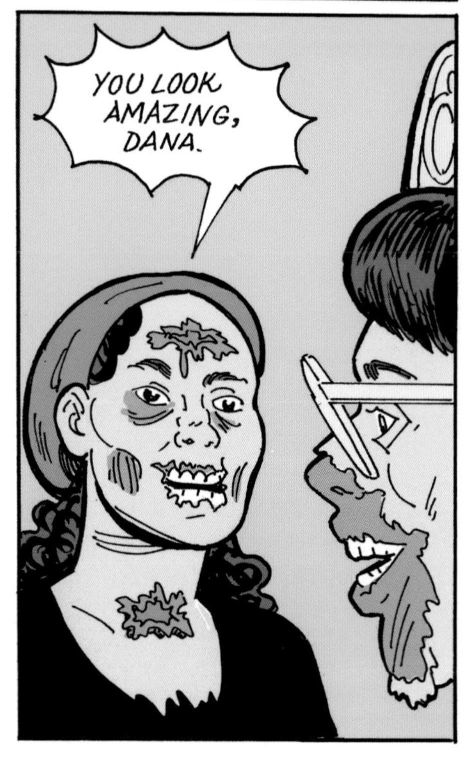
YOU LOOK AMAZING, DANA.

YOU LOOK... DELICIOUS.

CHANGE CAN'T WAIT

WIND
OWER
NOW

WHAT DO WE WANT?
CLIMATE ACTION!

EXCUSE ME! SORRY.
CLIMAT

EXCUSE ME!

GOLF
CASINO
ARCADE
ICE CREAM

IT IS MY HONOR TODAY, AS MAYOR OF THIS GREAT CITY, TO KICK OFF THE SEVENTEENTH ANNUAL BOCA BELLA MERMAID PARADE BY CROWNING OUR MERMAID QUEEN.

THIS YEAR'S QUEEN HAS MADE A SIGNIFICANT CONTRIBUTION TO THE ISLAND'S TOURISM INDUSTRY BY ESTABLISHING THE BOCA BELLA HOTEL ASSOCIATION...

LET'S HEAR A ROUND OF APPLAUSE FOR MRS. CLARISSA STUBBS.

ACTION!
WHAT DO WE WANT?
CLIMATE ACTION!

WHEN DO WE WANT IT?
NOW!

WE HAVE A DISTURBANCE AT THE MAYOR'S FLOAT. I NEED ALL AVAILABLE PERSONNEL FOR BACKUP.

FILM FOR ME?

FIRST OF ALL, THANK YOU. I NEVER THOUGHT I'D BE QUEEN OF ANYTHING.

I'M ABOUT TO GRADUATE HIGH SCHOOL. WELL, I HOPE I GRADUATE. LONG STORY.

ANYWAY, UH, HONESTLY, I'M PISSED OFF.

I'M SEVENTEEN, AND ON TOP OF WORRYING ABOUT COLLEGES AND JOBS AND BOYS, I WAKE UP EVERY MORNING AND READ ABOUT FORESTS BURNING AND GLACIERS MELTING AND WHALES GOING EXTINCT.
ICE CREAM
FUNLAND
MINI GOLF
ARCADE

ALRIGHT. I THINK YOU'VE MADE YOUR POINT.
LET HER SPEAK!
CLIMATE ACTION

LET HER SPEAK!
LET HER SPEAK!
LET HER SPEAK!
LET HER SPEAK!

THE PLANET IS LITERALLY ON FIRE. AND THE WORST PART IS, IT DOESN'T EVEN HAVE TO BE THIS WAY.

POLI
POLI
POL

I AM ORDERING YOU TO DISPERSE IMMEDIATELY.
SNACKS
ICE CREAM
NOW

ANYONE WHO REMAINS MAY BE ARRESTED OR SUBJECT TO OTHER POLICE ACTION, INCLUDING CHEMICAL AGENTS, BATONS, OR ANY OTHER FORCE DEEMED NECESSARY.

CRACK

CLIMATE ACTION

THEY'RE TRYING TO PEN US IN AND ARREST US. WE NEED TO GET OUT OF HERE.
FOLLOW ME!

TICKETS
MINI GOLF EXPERIENC
SALE
50% OFF
PHAROAH'S TOMB
HAUNTED HOUSE

WHOOSH

CRUNCH

CRACK

DANA! LOOK OUT!

CRASH

COME ON! HURRY.
Diner

BUZZ

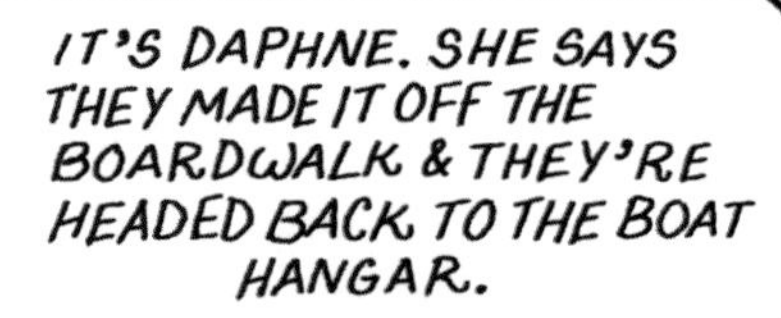
IT'S DAPHNE. SHE SAYS THEY MADE IT OFF THE BOARDWALK & THEY'RE HEADED BACK TO THE BOAT HANGAR.

PHEW!
OPEN

DANA?
OH! UH...
HI. I'M ANDREAS.

ANDREAS IS VISITING FROM COLLEGE. WE MET AT AN ANCHORWATCH MEETING.

THESE ARE MY FRIENDS FROM SCHOOL, BRADEN, LILY AND WYE.
SEAT YOURSELF

WERE YOU DOING A SHOOT?

WE CRASHED THE MERMAID PARADE AND THINGS GOT CRAZY. WE WERE THIS CLOSE TO GETTING ARRESTED.

NO WAY.
LOOK.

ALRIGHT, I THINK YOU'VE MADE YOUR POINT.
LET HER SPEAK.

LET HER SPEAK!
LET HER SPEAK!
CLIMATE

THE PLANET IS LITERALLY ON FIRE. AND THE WORST PART IS, IT DOESN'T EVEN HAVE TO BE THIS WAY.

I CAN'T BELIEVE YOU HAD THE GUTS TO DO THAT.
NEITHER CAN I.

WHAT ARE YOU UP TO NOW?
BACK TO EDITING. WE JUST STOPPED FOR A COFFEE BREAK.

ARE YOU COMING TO THE FILM FESTIVAL?
DO YOU WANT ME THERE?

YEAH. COME SUFFER WITH US.
IT'S GONNA BE HELLA AWKWARD.

YOU SHOULD COME TOO.

I'D LOVE TO, BUT I'M, UH, FLYING BACK TO NEW YORK TOMORROW NIGHT.
OH.

I GOTTA BOUNCE. I'LL SEE YOU AT SCHOOL.
HEY! WAIT FOR US.

BYE, DANA! BYE, NEW GUY.

YOU DIDN'T TELL ME YOU WERE LEAVING SO SOON.
I WAS HAVING SO MUCH FUN, I KIND OF FORGOT.

LOOKS LIKE IT'S CLEARING UP. WANNA TAKE A WALK?
RIGHT NOW?
WHY NOT?

CLIMATE A

GOD, I LOVE THESE TREES.

I WAS DESPERATE TO LEAVE FLORIDA, AND NOW I KIND OF MISS IT.
ARE YOU KIDDING? YOU ARE **SO** LUCKY YOU GOT OUT.

I'D NEVER WANT TO MOVE BACK HERE, BUT COMING HOME TO VISIT, I LOVE ALL THE TACKY STUFF I USED TO HATE, THE SOUVENIR STORES, THE SKETCHY THEME PARKS, THE STRIP MALLS.

NO WAY. NOPE. NEVER. NOT ME.

JUST WAIT. YOU'LL SEE WHAT I MEAN.

WHERE HAVE YOU BEEN? I'VE BEEN TEXTING FOR HOURS.

I WAS AT THE CLIMATE MARCH. WHEN THE STORM BROKE, WE WENT TO TASTY FREEZE TO WAIT IT OUT.

WHO'S WE?
ME AND ANDREAS. THE BOY I WAS TELLING YOU ABOUT. WE HAD PIE AND COFFEE AND JUST TALKED.

IT'S AFTER MIDNIGHT.
WE GOT A LOT OF REFILLS.

YOU'VE BEEN MY DAUGHTER FOR SEVENTEEN YEARS. YOU THINK I CAN'T TELL WHEN YOU'RE LYING? DRY OFF AND GO TO SLEEP. I'LL DRIVE YOU TO SCHOOL IN THE MORNING.

CHAPTER NINE

I WAS WORRIED WHAT PRINCIPAL LOBLAW WOULD DO WHEN SHE SAW THE NEWS, BUT SHE JUST TOLD ME THERE'S A DIFFERENCE BETWEEN GOOD TROUBLE AND BAD TROUBLE.

JEANINE GAVE ME A "B" ON MY DOCUMENTARY. SHE SAID THE FAST CUTS CREATED A SENSE OF URGENCY, WHICH FIT THE TONE OF THE MATERIAL, BUT THAT I NEEDED TO WORK ON MY FRAMING.

IN THIRD PLACE IS "BANYAN STREET BLUES" BY ARNOLD PARK.
IN SECOND PLACE IS "SANDCASTLE SUMMER" BY ANDREA FELDSTEIN.
FILM FESTIVAL

AND THE WINNER OF THE SHORT FILM CATEGORY IN THIS YEAR'S BOCA BELLA FILM FESTIVAL IS...

"OUT OF WATER," DIRECTED BY LILY VILLASEÑOR.

LILY KILLED IT. YOU NEVER DOUBTED HER, DID YOU? SHE'S A SERIOUS ARTIST. THAT DOESN'T MEAN SHE WON'T HAVE HARDSHIPS, BUT INSTEAD OF WISHING THEM ON HER, I WAS READY TO CELEBRATE HER SUCCESS.
SHORT FILMS
COMING SOON

I'D COME TO TERMS WITH STAYING IN BOCA BELLA A BIT LONGER, AND HAD JUST STARTED A JOB SEARCH, WHEN I GOT AN UNEXPECTED EMAIL.

I DON'T KNOW IF I'M GONNA TAKE IT.
WHY WOULDN'T YOU?
WHO'S GOING TO BABYSIT?

MRS. AVILA'S DAUGHTER ROSE OPENED A HOME DAYCARE. IT'S CHEAPER THAN THE YMCA AND JESSE KNOWS ROSE.

WHERE WILL I LIVE? THE INTERNSHIP PAYS ALMOST NOTHING AND RENT IN NEW YORK IS INSANE.
YOUR COUSIN ALBERT AND HIS WIFE LIVE IN PARK SLOPE. YOU COULD STAY WITH THEM FOR A WHILE.

I DIDN'T REALIZE YOU WERE SO EAGER TO GET RID OF ME.
I'M NOT TRYING TO GET RID OF YOU. I JUST KNOW HOW BAD YOU WANT TO LEAVE BOCA BELLA.

IT'S NOT BECAUSE OF YOU, YOU KNOW.
GET OVER HERE. YOUR CAP IS ON CROOKED.

WE HAD OUR GRADUATION CEREMONY AND THEN A PARTY ON THE BEACH. BY JUNE, THERE WAS ONLY A BIT OF A LINGERING FISH STENCH.

I DIDN'T KNOW WHEN WE'D SEE EACH OTHER AGAIN, AND I WANTED TO REMEMBER MY FRIENDS THIS WAY FOREVER. SILLY. WILD. POWERFUL AS OCEAN WAVES.

9:10
NEW YORK

KEEP YOUR HEADPHONES ON AND DON'T TALK TO ANYBODY.
I DON'T WANT TO TALK TO ANYBODY.

IF SOMEONE TRIES TO SELL YOU SOMETHING, JUST IGNORE THEM.
I WON'T EVEN MAKE EYE CONTACT.

I GOT YOU SOMETHING.
YOU DIDN'T HAVE TO DO THAT.

IT'S NOT MUCH, BUT I THOUGHT YOU COULD USE IT.

OH. IT'S DEODORANT.
FIGHTS ODOR!

THERE'S OTHER STUFF IN THERE- SOAPS AND LOTION. SOME LITTLE SHAMPOO BOTTLES.
THANKS, JO. THAT WAS REALLY NICE OF YOU.

ONE IS LAVENDER, THE OTHER IS PEACHES AND CREAM. I WASN'T SURE WHICH SCENT YOU'D LIKE BEST.
THEY BOTH SOUND GREAT. THANK YOU.

YOU'VE GOT A BLUE MUSTACHE.

FOR ME? THANKS, KIDDO. I'LL SEE YOU SOON.

THIS IS BLUE BOLT BUS NUMBER ONE-FIVE-OH-FIVE WITH OVERNIGHT SERVICE TO MANHATTAN.

ALL UNCHECKED BAGGAGE MUST FIT INTO A LUGGAGE COMPARTMENT OR BE STOWED UNDER THE SEAT IN FRONT OF YOU. BLUE BOLT IS NOT RESPONSIBLE FOR LOST OR STOLEN ITEMS.

I WAS LOST / I WAS SCARED/ NOW I'M STRONG SO YOU BETTER BE PREPARED/ I'M A MONSTER/ M-M-M-M MONSTER/
HALL

BLUE BOLT

ALL UNCHECKED BAGGAGE MUST FIT INTO A LUGGAGE COMPARTMENT OR BE STOWED UNDER THE SEAT IN FRONT OF YOU. BLUE BOLT IS NOT RESPONSIBLE FOR LOST OR STOLEN ITEMS.

I WAS LOST / I WAS SCARED/ ♪
NOW I'M STRONG SO YOU BETTER BE
PREPARED/ I'M A MONSTER/
M-M-M-M MONSTER/ ♪
HALL

BLUE
BOLT

REAL LIFE DOESN'T FOLLOW A THREE-ACT STRUCTURE. IT MEANDERS LIKE A STREAM OR SPIRALS LIKE A SNAIL'S SHELL. SOMETIMES THINGS GET BROKEN THAT CAN NEVER BE FIXED. AND SOMETIMES WHAT SEEMS LIKE THE END IS JUST THE BEGINNING.

ACKNOWLEDGMENTS

Greg Hunter and Kimberly Morales at Lerner Books; Lane Milburn; the Fleischer family; Alejandra Oliva; Yogi Gamester; Terry and Mark Kamikawa; Cecilia Jonsson-Bisset; Leslie, Suraj, and Nisha Dubey; Mariana and Grace Alzamora; Max Morris; Conor Stechschulte and Maire O'Neill; Chris Day and Molly Colleen O'Connell; Kenny Rasmussen; Eric Watts, Lauren Edwards and Lee; Jill Flanagan; Jules Zinn; Shea Cahill; Seth Sher, Heather Gabel, and Evelyn; Fiona Cook, Nicholas Efrosinis, Icarus, Orpheus, and the McKinley Park Community Garden; Ruth Oppenheim-Rothschild; David and Christine Wolf; Annie Koyama; my students.

ABOUT THE AUTHOR

Anya Davidson is a cartoonist and musician living in Chicago. She is the author of three other graphic novels, including *School Spirits* (PictureBox Inc., 2014) and *Band For Life* (Fantagraphics Books, 2016).